D0490455

The Book of Chameleons

José Eduardo Agualusa was born in Huambo, Angola in 1960. For a number of years he lived in Rio de Janeiro and now spends most of his time between Lisbon and Luanda where his wife and two young children live. Agualusa's first work of fiction, *The Conspiracy*, a historical novel set in Sao Paulo de Luanda between 1880 and 1911, paints a fascinating portrait of a society marked by opposites, in which only those who can adapt have any chance of success. Other novels include *The Market of the Damned* (1992) and *The Rainy Season*, which depicts the devastating history of an Angola tormented by thirty years of civil war. He has also published three books of short stories and *At the Heart of the Forests*, a poetry collection. His novel *Creole* (Arcadia), which has evoked comparisons to Bruce Chatwin's *The Viceroy of Ouidah*, was awarded the Portuguese Grand Prize for Literature, and is a bestseller in Angola, Brazil, France, Germany, Italy, Portugal and Spain (including its Catalan translation). *Lisboa Africana*, produced in collaboration with Fernando Semedo and photographer Elza Rocha, is a much-lauded volume about Lisbon's African community. He's now working on his 7th novel.

Daniel Hahn has translated José Eduardo Agualusa's novel *Creole* (Arcadia), and the autobiography of Brazilian footballer Pelé. He is the author of a work of narrative history, *The Tower Menagerie*, and the editor of several reference books including a series of reading guides for children, *The Ultimate Book Guides*. As a freelance writer and researcher he has worked regularly with Shakespeare's Globe and Oxford University Press. He is a member of the Globe Council, and of the London Committee of Human Rights Watch. He is currently editorial director of ICONS, a cultural website (www.icons.org.uk).

José Eduardo Agualusa

The Book
of Chameleons

Translated from the Portuguese by Daniel Hahn

ARCADIA BOOKS
LONDON

Arcadia Books Ltd
15-16 Nassau Street
London W1W 7AB

www.arcadiabooks.co.uk

First published in the United Kingdom 2006
Originally published by Publicações Dom Quixote, Lisbon, 2004
Copyright © José Eduardo Agualusa and Publicações Dom Quixote, 2004
By arrangement with Dr Ray-Güde Mertin, Literarische Agentur, Bad Homburg, Germany

This English translation from the Portuguese, *O vendedor de passados*
Copyright © Daniel Hahn, 2006

José Eduardo Agualusa has asserted his moral right to be identified as the author of this work in
accordance with the Copyright, Designs and Patents Act, 1988.

A catalogue record for this book is available from the British Library

ISBN 1-905147-15-5

Typeset in Bembo by Basement Press
Printed in Finland by WS Bookwell

Arcadia Books supports English PEN, the fellowship of writers who work together to promote
literature and its understanding. English PEN upholds writers' freedoms in Britain and around
the world, challenging political and cultural limits on free expression.
To find out more, visit www.englishpen.org or contact
English PEN, 6-8 Amwell Street, London EC1R 1UQ

Arcadia Books distributors are as follows:

in the UK and elsewhere in Europe:
Turnaround Publishers Services
Unit 3, Olympia Trading Estate
Coburg Road London N22 6TZ

in the USA and Canada:
Independent Publishers Group
814 N. Franklin St. Chicago, IL 60610

in Australia:
Tower Books
PO Box 213 Brookvale, NSW 2100

in New Zealand:
Addenda
Box 78224 Grey Lynn Auckland

in South Africa:
Quartet Sales and Marketing
PO Box 1218 Northcliffe Johannesburg 2115

Arcadia Books is the *Sunday Times* Small Publisher of the Year

'If I were to be born again, I'd like to be something completely different. I'd quite like to be Norwegian. Or Persian, perhaps. Not Uruguayan, though – that'd feel too much like just moving down the street...'

Jorge Luis Borges

A Little Night-Time God

I was born in this house, and grew up here. I've never left. As it gets late I press my body against the window and look at the sky. I like watching the flames, the racing clouds, and above them, angels – hosts of angels – shaking down the sparks from their hair, flapping their broad fiery wings. The sight is always the same. But every evening I come here and I enjoy it, and I'm moved by it, as if seeing it for the very first time. Last week Félix Ventura arrived earlier than usual and surprised me in the act of laughing at a massive cloud – out there in the tempestuous blue – that was dashing about in circles, like a dog trying to put out the fire in his tail.

'I don't believe it – are you laughing?'

The creature's amazement annoyed me. I was afraid – but I didn't move, not a muscle. The albino took off his dark glasses, put them away in the inside pocket of his jacket, took the jacket off – slowly, sadly – and hung it carefully on the back of a chair. He chose a vinyl record and put it on the deck of the old player. *Acalanto para um Rio*, 'Lullaby for a River', by Dora, the Cicada, a Brazilian singer who I imagine must have had some sort of reputation in the seventies. I'm assuming this because of the record sleeve, which shows a beautiful black woman in a bikini, with big butterfly wings fixed to her back. 'Dora, the Cicada – *Acalanto para um Rio* – today's smash hit.' Her voice burns in the air. These past weeks this has been the soundtrack to our evenings. I know the words by heart.

Nothing passes, nor expires,
The past is now

A river, sleeping –
Memory tells
A thousand lies.

The river waters are asleep
And in my arms
The days are sleeping –
Sleep the wounds,
The agonies.

Nothing passes, nor expires,
The past is now
A sleeping river,
Seeming dead, just barely breathing –
But rouse it and it bursts to life.

Félix waited until the light faded, and the final notes from the piano faded too; then he turned one of the sofas, almost soundlessly, till it was facing the window. At last he sat down. He stretched out his legs, with a sigh...

'*Pópilas!*' he exclaimed. 'So I see Your Lowness is laughing?! That's quite a novelty...'

As I looked at him, he seemed worn out. He brought his face close to mine, and I could see his bloodshot eyes. His breath swamped my whole body. Acidic, and warm.

'You've really got terrible skin, you know that? We must be related...'

I'd been expecting something like that. If I'd been able to speak I would have answered him back. But my vocal abilities extend only to laughing. All the same I did try to aim a sort of fierce guffaw at his face, a sound that might succeed in alarming him, to get him away from me – but all I managed was a sort of flimsy gurgling. Until last week the albino had always ignored me. But since then, since he heard me laughing, he's started coming home earlier; he goes to the kitchen and comes back with a glass of papaya juice, he sits on the sofa, and shares the sunset rites with me. We talk. Or rather, he talks, I listen. Sometimes I laugh – this seems enough for him. I get the sense that there's already a thread of friendship holding us together. On Saturday nights – but not always – the albino arrives with some girl. They're slender girls, tall and supple, with thin heron legs. Some of them are scared as they come in, they sit on the edge of their chair, trying not to look directly at him, unable to hide their disgust. They have a soft drink, sip by sip, and then in silence they undress; they wait for him lying on their backs, arms crossed over their breasts. Others – bolder – will wander around the house on their own, assessing the shine on the silver, the antique quality of the furniture, but they quickly come back to the living room, alarmed at the stacks of books in the bedrooms and the corridors, and more alarmed still at the fierce gaze of the men in top hats and monocles, the playful gaze of the *bessanganas*, those bourgeois women of Luanda and Benguela, the astonished stare of the officers from the Portuguese navy in their ceremonial outfits, the wild stare of a nineteenth-century Congolese prince, the challenging stare of a famous black North American writer – each of them in golden frames, posing for all eternity. They look around the bookcases for records:

'Don't you have any *cuduro* music, old man?'

And since the albino doesn't have any *cuduro*, he doesn't have any *quizomba*, he doesn't have the Banda Maravilha or Paulo Flores – the greatest hits of the day – they end up choosing something with a bright cover, which usually means it's some Cuban rhythms or other. They dance, slowly embroidering small steps across the wooden floor, as the shirt buttons come undone, one by one. That perfect skin, so very black, moist and radiant, against the albino's – dry, rough, and pinkish. I watch it all. In this house I'm like a little night-time god. During the day, I sleep.

The House

This is a living house. A living, breathing house. I hear it sighing, all night long. The wide brick and wooden walls are always cool, even in the heat of the day when the sun has silenced the birds, lashed at the trees, and begun to melt the tarmac. I slip across them like a tick on its host's skin. As I hold them I feel a heart beating. Mine, perhaps, or that of the house. It hardly matters. It does me good. It makes me feel safe. Sometimes Old Esperança will bring along one of her smaller grandchildren. She carries them on her back, wrapped tightly in a piece of cloth, as is the ancient custom of the country. She does all her work like this. She sweeps the floor, dusts down the books, cooks, washes clothes, does the ironing. And the baby, its head pressed in to her back, feels her warmth and her heartbeat, believes itself to be back in its mother's womb, and sleeps. My relationship with the house is just the same. As I've said, as it gets late I stay in the living room, pressed up against the windowpanes, watching the dying sun. Once night has fallen I wander from area to area – the living room opens out to the garden, a narrow, badly-tended sort of thing, which is only delightful thanks to the two glorious Imperial palm trees, very tall, very haughty, that stand at either end, keeping watch over the house. The living room leads to the library. A wide doorway takes you from the library into the corridor, which is a deep tunnel, damp and dark, that gets you to the bedroom, the dining room, the kitchen. This part of the house faces out towards the yard. The morning light strokes the walls – green, gentle, filtered through the tall foliage of the avocado tree. At the end of the corridor, on your left as you come in from the living room, a small staircase rises as if with some effort in three broken flights of steps. If you go up the staircase you'll find yourself in a sort of garret, where the albino goes only rarely. It's full of crates of books. I'm not often there myself either. Bats sleep upside-down on the walls, wrapped in their black capes. I don't know whether geckos are part of a bat's diet. And I prefer not to know. It's the same thing – terror, that is – that keeps me from exploring the yard. From the windows of the kitchen, the dining room or Félix's room I can see the wild grasses growing untamed between the rosebushes. A huge, leafy avocado tree rises up in the exact centre of the yard. There are two tall medlar trees too, laden with fruit, and at least ten papaya trees. Félix believes in the restorative powers of papaya. The garden is closed off by a tall wall, the top of which is studded with shards of glass in different colours, held in place by cement. From my vantage point they look like teeth. This fierce device doesn't prevent boys from occasionally climbing the wall to steal avocadoes, medlar fruit and papayas. They put a wooden board on the top of the wall, and pull themselves over. If you ask me it's far too risky an enterprise for such meagre pickings. But perhaps they're not doing it in order to savour the fruit, but to savour the risk itself... Maybe all risks will taste to them of ripe medlar fruit from now on. You can imagine that one of them will end up becoming a sapper. There will always be more than enough work for sappers in this country. Only yesterday I saw something on television, a report on the mine-sweeping operations. The director of an NGO was bemoaning how uncertain they are about numbers. No one knows with any certainty how many mines were buried in Angolan soil. Somewhere between ten and twenty million. More mines than Angolans, probably. So say one of these boys becomes a sapper. Whenever he drags himself across a minefield he'll always have that faint taste of medlar fruit in his mouth. And one day he'll be faced with the inevitable question, thrown at him by a foreign journalist with mingled curiosity and horror:

'So when you're there disarming a mine, what goes through your head?'
And the boy he still has within him will reply, with a smile:
'Medlar fruit, old man.'
Old Esperança thinks it's the wall that makes the thieves – I've heard her say as much to Félix. The albino turned to her, amused:
'Who'd have thought I had an anarchist in the house?! Any moment now I'm going to discover that you've been reading Bakunin...'

He said this, then forgot all about her. She'd never read Bakunin, of course; never read a book at all, come to that, barely knows how to read. But I'm always learning things about life in general, or life in this country – which is life in a state of intoxication – from hearing her talk to herself, sometimes in a gentle murmur, almost like a song, sometimes out loud like someone scolding, as she cleans the house. Old Esperança believes that she's never going to die. In 1992 she survived a massacre. She'd gone to the house of one of the opposition leaders to pick up a letter from her youngest son who was on service in Huambo, when bursts of gunfire suddenly erupted from all around. She was determined to leave the place, to go back to her old *musseque* house, but they wouldn't let her.

'It's a crazy idea, old lady. Just pretend that it's raining. It'll pass soon enough.'

But it didn't pass. Like a storm the gunfire gathered, getting more ferocious and closing in, getting louder and closer to the house. Félix was the one who told me what happened that night:

'This brawling band, a mob of rioters, well armed and extremely drunk, forced their way into the house and slapped around all the people there. The commander wanted to know the name of the old woman. *Esperança Job Sapalalo, sir*, she said, and he laughed. *Esperança – Hope*, he joked. *Always the last to die.* The opposition leader and his family were lined up in the yard and shot. When it came to be Old Esperança's turn, the gunmen had no bullets left. *You know what saved you, don't you?* the commander shouted – *it was logistics. We've never been very good with logistics.* And he sent her on her way. Since then she's believed herself to be immune to death. And who knows, maybe she is.'

It doesn't strike me as impossible. Esperança Job Sapalalo has a fine web of wrinkles on her face and completely white hair, but her flesh is still firm, her gestures solid and precise. If you ask me she's the pillar keeping this house up.

The Foreigner

Félix Ventura studies the newspapers as he has his dinner, leafing through them carefully, and if an article catches his eye he marks it with his pen, in lilac-coloured ink. Once he's done eating he cuts it out and stores it carefully away in a file. On one of the shelves in the library he has dozens of these files. Another is where his hundreds of video cassettes lie. Félix likes to record news bulletins, important political happenings, anything that might one day be useful to him. The tapes are lined up in alphabetical order, by the name of the person or the event they're about. His dinner consists of a bowl of vegetable broth, a speciality of Old Esperança's, a cup of mint tea, and a thick slice of papaya, dressed with lemon and a dash of port wine. In his room, before going to bed, he puts on his pyjamas with such an air of formality that I'm always half-expecting him to tie a sombre-looking tie around his neck. But on this particular night, the shrill ring of the doorbell interrupted him as he ate his soup. This irritated him. He folded up his paper, got up with some effort and went to open the door. I saw a tall man come in, distinguished looking, a hooked nose, prominent cheekbones, and a generous moustache, curved and gleaming, the kind people haven't had these past hundred years. His eyes were small and bright, and seemed to take possession of everything they saw. He was wearing a blue suit, in an old-fashioned cut but which suited him, and in his left hand he was holding a document case. The room darkened. It was as though night – or something even more grief-stricken than night – had come in with him. He took out a calling card, and read aloud:

15

'*Félix Ventura. Guarantee your children a better past.*' And he laughed. A sad laugh, but not unpleasant. 'That would be you, I presume? A friend of mine gave me your card.'

I couldn't place his accent. He spoke softly, with a mix of different pronunciations, a faint Slavic roughness, tempered by the honeyed softness of the Portuguese from Brazil. Félix Ventura took a step back:

'And who are you?'

The foreigner closed the door. He walked around the room, his hands clasped behind his back, pausing for a long moment in front of the beautiful oil portrait of Frederick Douglass. Then he sat down, at last, in one of the armchairs, and with an elegant gesture invited the albino to do the same. It was as though he were the owner of the house. Certain common friends, he said – his voice becoming even gentler – had given him this address. They'd told him of a man who dealt in memories, a man who sold the past, clandestinely, the way other people deal in cocaine. Félix looked at him with mistrust. Everything about this strange man annoyed him – his manners that were both gentle and authoritative, his ironic way of speaking, the antiquated moustache. He sat himself down in a grand wickerwork chair, at the opposite end of the room, as though afraid the other man's delicacy might be contagious.

'And might I know who you are?'

Again his question received no reply. The foreigner asked permission to smoke. He took a silver cigarette case from the pocket of his jacket, opened it, and rolled a cigarette. His eyes skipped one way and another, his attention distracted, like a chicken pecking around in the dust. And then he smiled with unexpected brilliance:

'But do tell me, my dear man – who are your clients?'

Félix Ventura gave in. There was a whole class, he explained, a whole new bourgeoisie, who sought him out. They were businessmen, ministers, landowners, diamond smugglers, generals – people, in other words, whose futures are secure. But what these people lack is a good past, a distinguished ancestry, diplomas. In sum, a name that resonates with nobility and culture. He sells them a brand new past. He draws up their family tree. He provides them with photographs of their grandparents and great-grandparents, gentlemen of elegant bearing and old-fashioned ladies. The businessmen, the ministers, would like to have women like that as their aunts, he went on, pointing to the portraits on the walls – old ladies swathed in fabrics, authentic bourgeois *bessanganas* –, they'd like to have a grandfather with the distinguished bearing of a Machado de Assis, of a Cruz e Souza, of an Alexandre Dumas. And he sells them this simple dream.

'Perfect, perfect.' The foreigner smoothed his moustache. 'That's what they told me. I require your services. But I'm afraid it may be rather a lot of work…'

'Work makes you free …' Félix muttered. It may be that he was just saying this to try and get a rise out of him, to test out the intruder's identity, but if that was his intention it failed – the foreigner merely nodded. The albino got up and disappeared in the direction of the kitchen. A moment later he returned with a bottle of good Portuguese wine that he held with both hands. He showed it to the foreigner, and offered him a glass. And he asked:

'And might I know your name?'

The foreigner examined the wine by the light of the lamp. He lowered his eyelids and drank slowly, attentively, happily, like someone following the flight of a Bach fugue. He put the glass down on a small table right in front of him, a piece of mahogany furniture with a glass cover; then finally straightened himself up and replied:

'I've had many names, but I mean to forget them all. I'd rather you were the one to baptize me.'

Félix insisted. He had to know – at the very least – what his clients' professions were. The foreigner raised his right hand – a broad hand, with long, bony fingers – in a vague gesture of refusal. But then he lowered it again, and sighed:

'You're right. I'm a photojournalist. I collect images of wars, of hunger and its ghosts, of natural disasters and terrible misfortunes. You can think of me as a witness.'

He explained that he was planning to settle in the country. He wanted more than just a decent past, a large family, uncles, aunts and cousins, nephews and nieces, grandfathers and grandmothers, including two or three *bessanganas*, now dead, of course (or perhaps living in exile somewhere?); he wanted more than just portraits and anecdotes. He needed a new name, authentic official documents that bore out this identity. The albino listened, horrified:

'No!' he managed to blurt out. 'I don't do things like that. I invent dreams for people, I'm not a forger… And besides, if you'll pardon my

17

bluntness, wouldn't it be a bit difficult to invent a completely African genealogy for you?'

'Indeed! And why is that?!...'

'Well – sir – ... you're white.'

'And what of it? You're whiter than I am...'

'White? Me?!' The albino choked. He took a handkerchief from his pocket and wiped his forehead. 'No, no! I'm black. Pure black. I'm a native. Can't you tell that I'm black?...'

From my usual post at the window I couldn't help giving a little chuckle at this point. The foreigner looked upwards as though he were sniffing the air. Tense – alert:

'Did you hear that? Who laughed just then?'

'Nobody,' the albino replied, and pointed at me. 'It was the gecko.'

The man stood up. He came up closer and I could feel his eyes on me. It was as though he were looking directly into my soul – my old soul. He shook his head slowly, in a baffled silence.

'Do you know what this is?'

'What?!'

'It's a gecko, yes, but a very rare species. See these stripes? It's a tiger gecko – a shy creature, we still know very little about them. They were first discovered half a dozen years ago in Namibia. We think they can live for twenty years – even longer, perhaps. They have this amazing laugh – doesn't it sound like a human laugh?'

Félix agreed. Yes, to begin with he'd also been disturbed by it. But then having consulted a few books about reptiles – he had them right there in the house, he had books about everything, thousands of them, inherited from his adopted father, a second-hand book dealer who'd exchanged Luanda for Lisbon a few months after independence – he'd discovered that there were certain species of gecko that produce sounds that are strikingly like laughter. They spent some time discussing me, which I found annoying – talking as if I weren't there! – and yet at the same time it felt as though they were talking not about me but about some alien being, some vague and distant biological anomaly. Men know almost nothing of the little creatures that share their homes. Mice, bats, ants, ticks, fleas, flies, mosquitoes, spiders, worms, silverfish, termites, weevils, snails, beetles. I decided that I might as well simply get on with my life. At that sort of time the albino's bedroom used to fill up with mosquitoes, and I was beginning to feel hungry. The foreigner stood up again, went over to the chair where he'd put the briefcase, opened it, and took out a thick envelope. He handed it to Félix, said his goodbyes, and went to the door. He opened it himself. He nodded, and was gone.

A Ship Filled with Voices

Five thousand dollars in large-denomination bills.

Félix Ventura tore open the envelope quickly, nervously, and the notes burst out like green butterflies – fluttered for a moment in the night air, then spread themselves all over the floor, the books, the chairs and sofas. The albino was getting anxious. He even went to open the door, meaning to chase after the foreigner, but out in the vast still night there was no sign of anyone.

'Have you seen this?!' He was talking to me. 'So now what am I supposed to do?'

He gathered the notes up one by one, counted them and put them back in the envelope – it was only then that he noticed that inside the envelope there was also a note; he read aloud:

'Dear Sir, I will be giving you another five thousand when I receive the material. I'm leaving you a few passport-style photos of myself for you to use on the documents. I'll come by again in three weeks.'

Félix lay down and tried to read a book – it was Nicholas Shakespeare's biography of Bruce Chatwin, in the Portuguese Quetzal edition. After ten minutes he put it down on the bedside table and got up again. He wandered round and round the house, muttering incoherent phrases, until dawn broke. His little widow's hands, tender and tiny, fluttered randomly about, independently, as he spoke. The tightly curled hair, trimmed down now, glowed around him with a miraculous aura. If someone had seen him from out on the road, seen him through the window, they would have thought they were looking at a ghost.

'No, what rubbish! I won't do it…'

[…]

'The passport wouldn't be hard to get, it wouldn't even be that risky, and it would only take a few days – cheap, too. I could do that – why not? I'll have to do it one day – it's the inevitable extension of what I'm doing anyway…'

[…]

'Take care, my friend, take care with the paths you choose to follow. You're no forger. Be patient. Invent some sort of excuse, return the money, and tell him it's not going to happen.'

[…]

'But you don't just turn down ten thousand dollars. I could spend two or three months in New York. I could visit the second-hand book dealers in Lisbon. I'll go to Rio, watch the samba dancers, go to the dancehalls, to the second-hand bookshops, or I'll go to Paris to buy records and books. How long has it been since I last went to Paris?'

[…]

Félix Ventura's anxiety disturbed my cynegetic activity. I'm a creature that hunts by night. Once I've tracked down my prey I chase them, forcing them up towards the ceiling. Once they're up there mosquitoes never come back down. I run around them, in ever decreasing circles, corral them into a corner and devour them. The dawn was already beginning to break when the albino – now sprawled on one of the living room sofas, began to tell me his life story.

'I used to think of this house as being a bit like a ship. An old steam ship heaving itself through the heavy river mud. A vast forest, and night all around.' Félix spoke quietly, and pointed vaguely at the outlines of his books. 'It's full of voices, this ship of mine.'

Out there I could hear the night slipping by. Something barking. Claws scratching at the glass. Looking through the window I could easily make out the river, the stars spinning across its back, skittish birds disappearing into the foliage. The mulatto Fausto Bendito Ventura, second-hand book collector, son and grandson of second-hand book collectors, awoke one Sunday morning to find a box outside his front door. Inside, stretched out on several copies of Eça de Queiroz's *The Relic*, was a little naked creature, skinny and shameless, with a glowing fuzz of hair, and a limpid smile of triumph. A widower with no children, the book collector brought the child into his home, raised him and schooled him, absolutely certain that there was some superior purpose that was plotting out this unlikely story. He kept the box, and the books that were in it too. The albino told me of it with pride.

'Eça,' he said, 'was my first crib.'

Fausto Bendito Ventura became a second-hand book collector quite without meaning to. He took pride in never having worked in his life. He'd go out early in the morning to walk downtown, *malembe-malembe* – slowly-slowly – all elegant in his linen suit, straw hat, bow tie and cane, greeting friends and acquaintances with a light touch of his index finger on the brim of his hat. If by chance he came across a woman of his generation he'd dazzle her with a gallant smile. He'd whisper: *Good day to you, poetry*... He'd throw spicy compliments to the girls who worked in the bars. It's said (Félix told me) that one day some jealous man provoked him:

'So what exactly is it that you do on working days?'

Fausto Bendito's reply – *all my days, my dear sir, are days off, I amble through them at my leisure*... – still provokes applause and laughter among the slim circle of old colonial functionaries who in the lifeless evenings of the wonderful Biker Beer-House still manage to cheat death, playing cards and exchanging stories. Fausto would lunch at home, have a siesta, and then sit on the veranda to enjoy the cool evening breeze. In those days, before independence, there wasn't yet the high wall separating the garden from the pavement, and the gate was always open. His clients needed only to climb a flight of stairs to have free access to his books, piles and piles of them, laid out at random on the strong living room floor.

Félix Ventura and I share a love (in my case a hopeless love) for old words. Félix Ventura was originally schooled in this by his father, Fausto Bendito, and then by an old teacher, for the first years of high school, a man subject to melancholic ways, and so slender that he seemed always to be walking in profile, like an old Egyptian engraving. Gaspar – that was the teacher's name – was moved by the helplessness of certain words. He saw them as down on their luck, abandoned in some desolate place in the language, and he sought to recover them. He used them ostentatiously, and persistently, which annoyed some people and unsettled others. I think he succeeded. His students started using these words too, to begin with merely in jest, but later like a private dialect, a tribal marking, which set them apart from their peers. Nowadays, Félix Ventura assured me, his students are still quite capable of recognising one another, even if they've never met before, on hearing just a few words...

'I still shudder each time I hear someone say 'duvet', a repulsive gallicism, rather than 'eiderdown', which to me (and I'm sure you'll agree with me on this) seems to be a very lovely, rather noble word. But I've resigned myself to 'brassiere'. 'Strophium' has a sort of historical dignity about it, but it still sounds a little odd – don't you think?'

Dream No. 1

I'm crossing a road in some alien city, making my way through the crowds of people. People of all races, all creeds, all sexes (for a long while I used to think there were just two…) pass me by. Men dressed in black, with dark glasses, carrying briefcases. Buddhist monks, laughing heartily, happy as oranges. Gossamer women. Fat matrons with shopping trolleys. Skinny adolescents on skates, slight birds slipping through the crowds. Little boys in single file, in school uniforms, each holding hands with the one in front, one teacher in the lead and another behind. Arabs in *djelabas* and skullcaps. Bald men walking killer dogs. Cops. Thieves. Intellectuals lost in thought. Workers in overalls. Nobody sees me. Not even the groups of Japanese, with their video cameras, and narrow eyes alert to everything around them. I stop right in front of people, I speak to them, I shake hands with them, but they take no notice of me. They don't speak to me. I've had this dream the last three nights. In an earlier life, my life still in human form, the same thing used to happen to me quite frequently. I remember waking up afterwards with a bitter taste in my mouth, my heart filled with anxiety. Back then I thought it was a premonition. Now I think it may be a confirmation. Either way, it no longer upsets me.

Alba

When she woke up, she was called Alba, or Aurora, or Lúcia. In the evening, she was Dagmar. At night: Estela. She was tall, very white – not that opaque, milky sort of white so common in northern European women, but with the light whiteness of marble, translucent, under which you could follow the impetuous flowing of her blood. Even before seeing her I was already afraid. When I did see her, I was speechless. Trembling, I handed her the folded envelope on the back of which my father had written *For Madame Dagmar*, in that ornate calligraphy that made any note, however simple, even a recipe for soup, look like a Caliph's decree. She opened it, and with her fingertips took out a small card, and as she looked at it she couldn't hide her laughter:

'You're a virgin?!'

I felt I was about to faint. Yes, I was turning eighteen, and I'd never had a woman. Dagmar led me by the hand through a maze of corridors, and I realised then that the two of us were now in an enormous room, haunted with sombre mirrors. Always smiling, she raised her arms and her dress slipped with a murmur to her feet:

'Chastity is a pointless agony, kid. And one I'm happy to fix…'

I imagined her with my father in the burning gloom of that same room. In a lightning-flash, in a revelation, I saw her, multiplied by the mirrors, undo her dress and release her breasts. I saw her wide hips, I felt her heat, and I saw my father, I saw my father's powerful hands. I heard his grown-man's laugh slapping against her skin, that vulgar language. I've lived that precise moment thousands, millions of times, with terror and revulsion. I lived it to the very end of my days.

I sometimes think of an unhappy line, I can't remember who it's by – I probably dreamed it. Maybe it's the chorus of a *fado*, or a tango perhaps, or some old samba I used to hear when I was a child.

'The worst of sins is not to fall in love.'

There were many women in my life – but I fear I didn't love any of them. Not passionately. Not, perhaps, as nature requires. I'm horrified to think of it. My current condition – and it torments me to believe this – is some sort of ironic punishment. Either that, or it was no more than a careless mistake.

The Birth of José Buchmann

This time the foreigner announced his arrival in advance – he telephoned and Félix Ventura had time to prepare himself for the meeting. By 7:30 he was dressed as though he were about to go to a wedding at which he himself were the groom, or father of the groom, in a light suit of coarse linen, on which a ruby-red silk tie glistened like an exclamation mark. He'd inherited the suit from his father.

'Are you expecting someone?'

Yes, he was expecting him. Old Esperança had left his fish soup in the oven so it wouldn't get cold. Early that morning she'd bought a lovely snapper, fresh from the Island fishermen, and three smoked catfish from the São Paulo market. A cousin had come from Gabela bringing some chilli-scented berries – *solid fire*, the albino explained to me – as well as manioc, sweet potato, spinach and tomatoes. No sooner had Félix put the dish out on the table than a powerful scent filled the room – warm as an embrace – and for the first time in ages I lamented my current condition. I'd like to be able to sit at the table too... The foreigner ate with a glowing appetite, as though he weren't tasting the firm flesh of the snapper but its whole life, the years and years slipping between the sudden explosions of a shoal, the whirling of the waters, the thick strands of light that on sunny evenings fall straight down into the blue abyss.

'It's an interesting exercise,' he said, 'to try and see things from the victim's point of view. This fish we're eating, for example... a fine snapper, isn't it?... Have you tried seeing our dinner from his point of view?'

Félix Ventura looked at the snapper with an attention that until that moment the fish hadn't deserved from him – then, horrified, he pushed his plate away. The other man continued uninterrupted:

'Do you think life expects us to be compassionate? I don't believe so. What life expects of us is that we celebrate. Let's return to the fish: if you were this fish, would you prefer me to be eating you with sadness or with delight?'

The albino kept his mouth shut. He knows he's a snapper (as we all are) but I think he'd rather not be eaten at all. The foreigner continued:

'Once I was taken to a party. There was this old man, and he was celebrating his hundredth birthday. I wanted to know how he was feeling. The poor man gave me an astonished smile, and said *I don't really know, it all happened so quickly...* He talked about his hundred years as though they were some disaster that had befallen him in the last few minutes. Sometimes I feel the same way. My soul hurts with too much past in it, and so much emptiness. I feel like that old man.'

He raised his glass:

'And still I'm alive. I've survived. I began to understand this – strange as it may seem to you – when I got off the boat in Luanda. To life! Angola has rescued me for life. To this propitious wine, which celebrates and unites.'

How old was he? Sixty perhaps, but if so he had looked after himself well – or forty, forty-five, but then he'd gone through some years of terrible despair... Looking at him as he sat there, I thought he looked as solid as a rhino. Those eyes of his seemed much older, filled with disbelief and fatigue, even though at certain points – like now when he was lifting his glass to drink a toast to Life – they lit up with the light of the dawn.

'How old are you?'

'Please allow me to be the one asking the questions. Were you able to do what I asked of you?'

Félix looked up. He had. He had an identity card, a passport, a driver's license, all these documents in the name of José Buchmann, native of Chibia, 52, professional photographer.

The town of São Pedro da Chibia, in the Huíla province to the south of the country, had been founded in 1884 by Madeiran colonists. But there were already half a dozen Boer families who were prospering there, raising cattle, farming the land, and praising God for the grace of having made them white in a country of black people – that's what Félix Ventura said, I'm just quoting him, of course. The clan was led by commander Jacobus Bothas. His lieutenant was a grim red-haired giant, Cornélio Buchmann, who in 1898 had married a Madeiran girl, Marta Medeiros, who gave him two sons. The elder of the two, Pieter, died in childhood; the younger, Mateus, was a famous hunter, who for years acted as guide to groups of South Africans and Englishmen who came to Angola in search of thrills. He was past fifty when he married an American artist, Eva Miller, and they had one son: José Buchmann.

Once they were done with dinner, and once he'd drunk his mint tea – José Buchmann preferred coffee – Félix Ventura went to fetch the cardboard folder and opened it onto the table. He showed the passport, the ID card, the driving license. There were various photos too. There was one, sepia-toned and well weathered, that showed a huge man with an absorbed air, sitting astride a gnu.

'This,' said the albino by way of introduction, 'is Cornélio Buchmann. Your grandfather.'

There was another showing a couple in an embrace, beside a river, with a broad, endless horizon in the background. The man had his eyes lowered. The woman, in a floral print dress, smiled at the camera. José Buchmann held the photo, and stood up so he was directly in the light of the lamp. His voice trembled a little.

'And these are my parents?'

The albino confirmed that yes, they were. Mateus Buchmann and Eva Miller, one sunny evening, beside the Chimpumpunhime river. It must have been José himself – then eleven years old – who'd captured that moment. He showed him an old issue of *Vogue*, with a report on big game hunting in southern Africa. The article was illustrated with a watercolour showing a wildlife scene – elephants bathing in a lake – signed by Eva Miller.

A few months after that photo had been taken, with the river rushing serenely towards its destination and the grasses high in the middle of the solemn evening, Eva left for Cape Town, on a trip which was due to last a month, and she never came back. Mateus Buchmann wrote to common friends in South Africa asking for news of his wife, and when he had no luck he left his son in the care of a servant, a blind old tracker, and set off to find her.

'And did he?'

Félix shrugged his shoulders. He gathered up the photographs, the documents, the magazine, and put them all away in the cardboard folder. He closed it, tying it with a thick red ribbon as though it were a gift, and handed it to José Buchmann.

'Forgive me for having to warn you,' he said. 'You really should keep away from Chibia.'

It's been nearly fifteen years that my soul has been trapped in this body, and I'm still not used to it. I lived for almost a century in the skin of a man, and I never managed to feel altogether human either. To this day I've known some thirty geckos, of five or six different species – I'm not sure exactly, I've never been all that interested in biology. Twenty of them grew rice, or built buildings, in vast China, or noisy India or Pakistan, before each one awoke from this first nightmare into this other which he or she (it hardly matters much) may find rather less appalling. Seven did the same – or something similar – in Africa; one was a dentist from Boston; one sold flowers in Belo Horizonte, in Brazil; the last had been a cardinal. He still missed the Vatican. Not one had read Shakespeare. The cardinal liked Gabriel García Márquez. The dentist told me he'd read Paulo Coelho. I've never read Paulo Coelho myself. But I'd gladly exchange the company of all the geckos and lizards for Félix Ventura and his long soliloquies. Yesterday he confided to me that he'd met an amazing woman. Though, he added, the word 'woman' doesn't quite do her justice.

'Ângela Lúcia is to women what humankind is to the apes.'

What an unpleasant phrase. But her name awoke in me memories of Alba, and all of a sudden I was alert and serious. His memory of this woman made him talkative. He talked about her like someone trying to give substance to a miracle...

'She's...' – he paused, his hands palms-up, eyes screwed shut in fierce concentration, finding the words – '... pure light!'

This seemed perfectly possible to me. A name can be a curse. Some are dragged along by their name, like muddy river waters after a heavy shower, however much they may resist they're propelled towards their destination... Others, on the contrary – their names are like masks that hide them, that deceive. Most have no power at all, of course. I recall my human name without any pleasure – but without pain either. I don't miss it. It wasn't me.

José Buchmann was a regular visitor to this strange ship. One more voice to add to all the others. He wanted the albino to add to his past. He didn't spare him any questions:

'What happened to my mother?'

My friend (for I believe I can now call him that) began to get fed up with his insistence. He'd done his job, and didn't feel any duty to do any more. But sometimes he'd acquiesce. Eva Miller – he said – never came back to Angola. An old client of his father's, from a southern family like the Buchmanns – old Bezerra – found her one evening, quite by chance, on a street in New York. A frail woman, already of some age, she moved through the throng of people with anxious slowness, 'like a little bird with a broken wing', Bezerra had said. At the corner she fell into his arms – literally fell into his arms – and the shock of it made him blurt out an expletive in Nhanheca. With a broad smile, the woman protested:

'That's not the sort of language you should be using with a lady!'

It was only then that he recognised her. The two of them sat at a café frequented by Cuban immigrants and talked until nightfall. At this point in the story, Félix paused.

'In New York night doesn't really fall – it lowers itself – here, yes, here it dives down from the sky.'

My friend set a lot of store by precision. Night dives down from the sky, he repeated, adding 'like a bird of prey'. Interruptions like this unsettled José Buchmann, who wanted to know how the story went on…

'And then?'

Eva Miller worked as an interior decorator. She lived alone in Manhattan, in a little apartment with a view of Central Park. The walls of the tiny living room, the walls of the sole bedroom, of the narrow corridor, were all covered with mirrors.

José Buchmann interrupted him…

'Mirrors?!'

Yes, my friend went on. But according to what old Bezerra had said, they weren't just ordinary mirrors. He smiled. I could tell that he was being pulled along by the force of his own story now. They were artefacts from the Hall of Mirrors at the funfair, warped panes each created with the cruel intention of capturing and distorting the image of anyone who dared to stand before it. A few had been given the power to transform the most elegant of creatures into an obese dwarf, others to stretch them out.

There were mirrors that could reveal a secret soul. Others that reflected not the face of the person looking into them, but the nape of their neck, their back. Glorious mirrors, and dreadful mirrors. In this way, whenever Eva Miller stepped into her apartment she didn't feel alone. When she appeared, a crowd appeared with her.

'Are you in touch with this Mr Bezerra?'

Félix Ventura looked at him, surprised. He shrugged his shoulders, as if to say – well, if you want me to go there I will... And he recounted how the old man had died in Lisbon just a few months earlier.

'Cancer,' he said. 'Lung cancer. He was a heavy smoker.'

They sat in silence, the two of them, thinking about Bezerra's death. The night was warm and humid. A calm breeze was blowing through the window. It brought with it many delicate, gentle mosquitoes, which flew about randomly, driven wild by the light. I was getting hungry. My friend looked over to the other man and smiled:

'I ought to be charging you overtime, damn it! Who do you think I am – Scheherezade?...'

Dream No. 2

There was a young man waiting for me, crouched by the wall. He opened his hands and I could see that they were filled with a furtive green glow, some enchanted substance that quickly disappeared into the darkness. 'Glow-worms', he whispered. There was a river flowing behind the wall, opaque and powerful, panting wearily like a watchdog. Beyond it the forest began. The low wall, in rough stone, allowed a view of the black water, the stars running along its back, the thick foliage in the background – as though in a well. The young man reached up to the top of the stones effortlessly, and after a moment's stillness, his head lost in the night, he climbed over to the other side. In the dream I was a man, still young, tall, but beginning to run to fat. I found it a bit of an effort getting up onto the wall. Then I jumped. I knelt down in the mud and the river came to lap at my hands.

'What's this?'

The boy didn't reply. He had his back to me. His skin was even darker than the night, smooth and lustrous, and on him too – as on the river – a whirligig of stars. I saw him advance towards the metallic waters, and disappear. He re-emerged, moments later, on the other bank. The river, lying at the feet of the forest, had finally gone to sleep. I remained, just sitting there, for some time, quite sure that if I could concentrate, if I could keep perfectly still, alert, if the brilliance of the stars could touch my soul – oh, I don't know – in some particular way, I would be able to hear the voice of God. And then I did really start to hear it, and it was hoarse and hissed like a kettle on the fire. I was struggling to understand what it was saying when out of the shadows – right in front of me – appeared a dog, a skinny setter, with a little radio, one of those pocket-radios, attached to its neck. It was badly tuned. A man's voice – deep, underground – was struggling against the storm of electric sounds:

'The worst of sins is not to fall in love,' said God, with the soft voice of a tango-singer: 'This broadcast has been sponsored by the Marimba Union Bakeries.'

The dog moved away then, limping slightly, and everything was silent again. I climbed the wall and left, heading towards the lights of the city. Before I'd reached the road I saw the young man again, crouched by the wall, his arms around the setter. The two of them looked at me as if they were a single being; I turned my back to them but I could still feel the challenging stare of the dog and the young man, as though there were something dark coming at me from behind. I awoke, startled. I was in a damp fissure in the wall. There were ants grazing between my fingers. I went out in search of the night. My dreams are almost always more lifelike than reality.

Splendorium

From the brilliant – but succinct – description my friend gave, I imagined a kind of illuminated angel. I imagined something with the brightness of a chandelier. I think Félix may have exaggerated a little. If she'd been at a party, lost amid the smoke and chaos, I wouldn't even have noticed her. Ângela Lúcia is a young woman, with dark skin and fine features, black braids falling loose on her shoulders. Vulgar. But yes, I must admit, occasionally – especially when she is moved or delighted – her skin does indeed sparkle with copper, and at these moments she's transformed, she's truly beautiful. But most of all I was struck by her voice, husky, but still humid, sensual. Félix arrived home that evening bringing her in with him like a trophy. Ângela Lúcia looked carefully at the books and the records. She laughed at the austere haughtiness of Frederick Douglass.

'And this guy, what's he doing here?'

'He's one of my great-grandfathers,' the albino replied. 'Great-grandfather Frederick, father to my paternal grandfather.'

The man had made his fortune in the nineteenth century selling slaves to Brazil. When the slave trade was ended he bought a farm in Rio de Janeiro where he lived many happy years. He returned to Angola an old man, bringing with him his two daughters, identical twins, then still young. Gossipers were soon spreading doubts about the likelihood of his paternity. The old man put paid to their lies quite happily by getting a servant-girl pregnant; and this time he did it with such talent that she gave birth to a son with eyes identical to his father's. He was even scared to look at him. The portrait was the work of a French painter. Ângela Lúcia asked whether she might be allowed to take a photograph of it. Then she asked whether she might be able to take a photograph of him – of my friend – sitting in the big wicker chair that his slave-trader great-grandfather had brought back with him from Brazil. The last of the evening light was dying softly on the wall behind him.

'I can't believe this light,' she said. 'I've never seen anything like it.'

Sometimes, she said, she could recognise a place just by the quality of the light. In Lisbon, the light at the end of spring leans madly over the houses, white and humid, and just a little bit salty. In Rio de Janeiro, in the season that the *carioca* locals instinctively call 'autumn', and that the Europeans insist disdainfully is just a figment of their imagination, the light becomes gentler, like a shimmer of silk, sometimes accompanied by a humid greyness, which hangs over the streets, and then sinks down gently into the squares and gardens. In the drenched land of the Pantanal in Mato Grosso, really early in the morning, the blue parrots cross the sky and they shake a clear, slow light from their wings, a light that little by little settles on the waters, grows and spreads and seems to sing. In the forests of Taman Negara in Malaysia, the light is like a liquid, which sticks to your skin, and has a taste and a smell. It's noisy in Goa, and harsh. In Berlin the sun is always laughing, at least during those moments when it manages to break through the clouds, like in those ecological stickers against nuclear power. Even in the most unlikely skies, Ângela Lúcia is able to discern shines that mustn't be forgotten; until she visited Scandinavia she'd believed that in that part of the world during the winter months light was nothing but the figment of people's imagination. But no, the clouds would occasionally light up with great flashes of hope. She said this, and stood up, adopting a dramatic pose:

'And Egypt? In Cairo? Have you ever been to Cairo?... To the pyramids of Giza?...' She lifted her hands and declaimed: 'The light, majestic, falls; so potent, so alive, that it seems to settle on everything like a sort of luminous mist.'

'That's Eça!' The albino laughed. 'I recognise him just by his adjectives – just like I can recognise Nelson Mandela just by his shirts. Presumably those are the notes he wrote during his trip to Egypt.'

Ângela Lúcia whistled happily, impressed; she clapped her hands. So was it true what they said about him, that he'd read the Portuguese classics from end to end, all of Eça, the inexhaustible Camilo? The albino coughed, flushed red. He changed the subject. He said he had a friend who like her was a photographer, and who – also like her – had lived many years abroad and had just returned to the country. A war photographer. Wouldn't she like to meet him?

'A war photographer?' Ângela looked at him with horror. 'What does that have to do with me? I'm not even sure that I am a photographer. I collect light.'

She took a plastic box out of her purse and showed it to the albino.

'It's my Splendorium,' she said. 'Slides.'

She always carries with her a few samples of these numerous kinds of splendour, gathered in the savannahs of Africa, in the old cities of Europe, or in the mountain ranges and forests of Latin America. Lights, flashes, faint glows, caught within a little plastic frame, which she uses to feed her soul in dark days. She asked if there was a projector somewhere in the house. My friend said yes, and went to fetch it. A few minutes later we were in Cachoeira, a little town in the Bahian Recôncavo.

'Cachoeira! I arrived there on a rickety old bus. I walked a little, my rucksack on my back, looking for a hostel, and found myself in this deserted little square. It was getting late. There was a tropical storm building in the east. The sun skimmed close to the earth, copper-coloured, until it clashed with that great wall of black clouds over beyond the old colonial mansions. It's a dramatic setting, don't you think?' She sighed. Her skin was alight, her lovely eyes filled with tears: 'And that is when I saw the face of God!'

A Gecko's Philosophy

Now, I've been studying José Buchmann for weeks. Watching him change. He isn't the same man who came into this house six, seven months ago. Something – something of the powerful nature of a metamorphosis – has been at work deep inside him. And perhaps it's like you see with a chrysalis, and the secret buzz of enzymes has been eating away at his organs. You could argue that we're all in a constant state of change. That's right, I'm not quite the same as I was yesterday either. The only thing about me that doesn't change is my past: the memory of my human past. The past is usually stable, it's always there, lovely or terrible, and it will be there forever.

(At least, this is what I thought before I met Félix Ventura.)

As we get old, the only certainty we're left with is that we will soon be older still. To describe someone as young seems to me to be rather misleading. Someone may be young, yes, but just in the same way that a glass is still intact moments before it shatters on the floor. But excuse my digression – that's what happens when a gecko starts philosophising... So let's get back to José Buchmann. I'm not suggesting that in a few days a massive butterfly is going to burst out of him, beating its great multicoloured wings. The changes I'm referring to are more subtle. For one thing, his accent is beginning to shift. He has lost – he is losing – that pronunciation somewhere between Slavic and Brazilian, that was rather sweet and sibilant, that bothered me so much to begin with. It has a Luandan rhythm to it now, better to match the silk print shirts and sports shoes that he's taken to wearing. I think he's become more expansive too. To hear him laugh you'd think he was Angolan. And he's lost that moustache too. He seems younger. That night he appeared at our door after almost a whole week away, and no sooner had the albino opened the door than he burst out with:

'I've been to Chibia!'

He was almost feverish. He sat in the great wicker throne that the albino's great-grandfather had brought from Brazil. He crossed his legs, then uncrossed them. He asked for a whisky. My friend, annoyed, poured him one. For God's sake, what ever made him go to Chibia?

'I went to visit my father's grave.'

'What?! The other man choked. Which father? You mean the fictional Mateus Buchmann?'

'My father! Mateus Buchmann may just be a fiction to you – albeit woven with tremendous class – but I assure you, the gravestone is quite real!'

He opened an envelope and took from it a dozen colour photographs that he spread onto the glass top of the little mahogany table. The first picture showed a cemetery; in the second, you could make out the tombstone on one of the graves: 'Mateus Buchmann / 1905-1978'. The others were pictures of the town.

a) Low houses.
b) Straight roads, opening widely into a green landscape.
c) Straight roads, opening widely into the immense tranquillity of a cloudless sky.
d) Chickens pecking around in the red dust.
e) An old mulatto man, sitting at a sad-looking bar table, his gaze resting on an empty bottle.
f) Withered flowers in a vase.
g) An enormous birdcage, without birds.
h) A pair of well worn boots, waiting on the doorstep of a house.

There was something dusky about all the photographs. It was the end or nearly the end – but who knew of what?

'I insisted, I warned you that you shouldn't go to Chibia!'

'I know. That's why I went…'

My friend shook his head. I couldn't tell if he was furious, or amused, or both. Slowly he studied the photograph of the tombstone. Then he smiled disarmingly:

'Good work. And I'm saying this as a professional: congratulations!'

Illusions

Early this morning I saw two boys in the yard imitating turtledoves. One was sitting astride a plank of wood, on the top of the wall, one leg on either side. The other had climbed into the avocado tree. He was collecting up avocadoes and throwing them over to the first, who caught them with the skill of a juggler and put them away into a bag. Then all of a sudden the one who was up in the tree, partly hidden by the leaves (I could only see his face and shoulders) raised his hands and cupped them to his mouth, and made a cooing sound. The other laughed, and copied him – it was like the birds themselves were right there, one on the wall and another on the highest branches of the avocado tree, the vigour of their song exorcising the last of the shadows. This episode reminded me of José Buchmann. When I saw him arrive in this house he sported the extraordinary moustache of a nineteenth-century gentleman, a dark suit of old-fashioned cut, as though he were a foreigner to all things. But now when I see him, as I do every other day, he comes into the house wearing a silk shirt, patterned in many colours, with the broad laugh and happy insolence of people native to this place. If I hadn't seen the two boys, if I'd only heard them, I would have sworn that there were turtledoves out there in the humid early morning. Looking at the past, considering it from where I am now, as I might look at a large screen in front of me, I can see that José Buchmann is not José Buchmann, but a foreigner imitating José Buchmann. But if I close my eyes to the past, and see him now, as though I'd never set eyes on him before, I simply would have to believe in him – this man has been José Buchmann all his life.

My first death didn't kill me

Once, when I was in my old human form, I decided to kill myself. I wanted to die, completely. I hoped that eternal life, Heaven and Hell, God, the Devil, reincarnation, all that stuff, was no more than slowly woven superstition, developed over centuries and centuries out of man's greatest terror. There was a gun shop right by my house but I'd never before set foot in it, and the owner didn't know me. There I bought a pistol. Then I bought a crime novel and a bottle of gin. Then I went down to a hotel on the beach, drank the gin in big gulps with considerable distaste (I've always found alcohol repulsive) and lay down on the bed to read the book. I thought that the gin, in combination with the tedium of a pointless plot, would give me the courage to put the gun to my head and pull the trigger. But as it turned out the book wasn't bad at all, and I kept reading right to the last page. By then it had started to rain. It was as though it were raining night – or to explain myself a little more clearly, it was as though falling from the sky were the thick fragments of that sleepy black ocean through which the stars navigate their course. I kept expecting the stars to fall and shatter on impact with the window, with a flash and a crashing. But they didn't fall. I turned out the light. I put the pistol to my head,

and I fell asleep.

Dream No. 3

I dreamt that Félix Ventura and I were having tea together. We were having tea, eating toast, and chatting. This was happening in a large *art nouveau* room, its walls covered in austere mirrors framed in jacaranda. A skylight with a lovely stained-glass window depicting two angels with open wings let in a lovely light. There were other tables around us, and other people seated at them, but they were faceless, or at least I didn't see their faces – it didn't matter to me, their whole existence was summed up in the soft murmuring I could hear. I could see myself reflected in the mirrors – a tall man, with a big, long face, well-built but weary, a little pale, with a barely concealed disdain for the rest of humanity. Yes, that was me, long ago, in the questionable glory of my thirties.

'You invented him, this strange José Buchmann, and now he's begun to invent himself. It's like a metamorphosis... A reincarnation... Or rather: a possession.'

My friend looked at me with alarm:

'What do you mean?'

'José Buchmann – surely you've noticed? – he's taken over the foreigner's body. He becomes more and more lifelike with each day that passes. And that man he used to be, that night-time character who came into our house eight months ago as though he'd come not from another country but from another time – where is he now?'

'It's a game. I know it's a game. We all know that.'

He poured himself some tea, and took two cubes of sugar, and stirred it. He drank, his eyes lowered. There we were, two gentlemen, two good friends, wearing white in an elegant café. We drank our tea, ate toast, and chatted.

'So be it,' I agreed. 'Let's acknowledge that it's no more than a game. So who is he?'

I wiped the sweat from my face. I've never distinguished myself by my valour. Maybe that's why I've never been attracted (speaking of my other life, that is) by the stormy destiny of heroes and rogues. I collected flick-knives. And with a pride of which I'm now ashamed I boasted about the exploits of a grandfather of mine who'd been a general. I did befriend some brave men, but unfortunately that didn't help me. Courage isn't contagious; fear is, of course. Félix smiled as he understood that my terror was greater, more ancient, than his:

'I have no idea. You?'

He changed the subject. He told me that a few days earlier he'd been at the launch of a new novel by a writer of the Angolan diaspora. He was an unpleasant sort of character, professionally indignant, who'd built up his whole career abroad, selling our national horrors to European readers. Misery does ever so well in wealthy countries. The man introducing him, a local poet and member of parliament for the ruling party, praised the new novel, its style, the vigour of the narrative, while at the same time criticising the writer for having a bogus take on our country's recent history. As soon as the discussion was opened up, another poet – he was a member of parliament too, and rather better known for his revolutionary past than for any literary activities – raised his hand:

'In your novels do you lie deliberately or just out of ignorance?'

Laughter. A murmur of approval. The writer hesitated a few seconds. Then counter-attacked:

'I'm a liar by vocation,' he shouted. 'I lie with joy! Literature is the only chance for a true liar to attain any sort of social acceptance.'

Then, more soberly, he added – his voice lowered – that the principal difference between a dictatorship and a democracy is that in the former there exists only one truth, the truth as imposed by power, while in free countries every man has the right to defend his own version of events. Truth, he said, is a superstition. He – Félix – was taken with this idea.

'I think what I do is really an advanced kind of literature,' he told me conspiratorially. 'I create plots, I invent characters, but rather than keeping them trapped in a book I give them life, launching them out into reality.'

I have a lot of sympathy for impossible passions. I am – or rather, I was – a specialist in them. Félix Ventura's slow siege of Ângela Lúcia moved me. Every morning he would send her flowers. She would complain about this, laughing, as soon as my friend had opened the door to her. Yes, of course they were wonderful, the porcelain roses with their exaggerated, artificial brilliance that made them seem rather like transvestites – or rather, *drag queens*; the orchids so lovely, though she preferred daisies, with their rustic beauty and lack of vanity. Yes, she thanked him for the flowers, but asked him please not to send any more because she didn't know what to do with them all. The air in her room in the Grande Hotel Universo was heavy, overwhelming, with so many discordant scents at once. The albino sighed. If he'd been able to he would have rolled out a rose-petal carpet at her feet. He would have liked to conduct an orchestra of birds to sing as rainbows appeared in the sky, one by one. Women are moved by declarations of love, however ridiculous they may be. Ângela Lúcia was moved. She kissed his face. Then she showed him the photographs she'd taken in the previous weeks: clouds.

'Aren't they like something out of a dream?'

Félix shuddered:

'I have dreams. Sometimes I have rather strange dreams. Last night I dreamt about him...'

And he pointed at me. I felt as though I were about to faint. I scuttled away, startled, to hide in a crack by the ceiling. Ângela Lúcia screamed, in one of those childish bursts of enthusiasm typical of her:

'A gecko?! How great!...'

'He isn't just any gecko. He's lived in this house for years. In the dream he had human form, a serious sort of man, with a face that seemed familiar to me. We were sitting in a café, chatting...'

'God gave us dreams so that we can catch a glimpse of the other side,' said Ângela Lúcia. 'To talk to our ancestors. To talk to God. And to geckos too, as it turns out.'

'Surely you don't believe that!?...'

'I most certainly do believe it. I believe in a lot of very strange things, my dear. If only you knew some of the things I believe, you'd look at me like a one-woman freak-show. So what did you talk about, then, you and this gecko?'

Spirit-scarers

Out there on the veranda, hanging from the ceiling, are dozens of ceramic charms to ward off spirits. Félix Ventura brought them back from his travels. Most are Brazilian. Birds painted in bright colours. Shells. Butterflies. Tropical fish. The legendary bandit Lampião and his happy band of hitmen. When the breeze makes them tremble they produce a clear murmur of water; this is why whenever the breeze blows, as it always does at this time, thank God, you are reminded of the character of this house:

A ship (filled with voices) moving up-river.

Something odd happened yesterday. Félix invited Ângela Lúcia and José Buchmann to dinner. I hid right at the top of one of the bookcases, from where I could easily see what was going on but certain that I couldn't be seen. José Buchmann arrived first. He came in, laughing, he and his shirt (printed with palm trees, parrots, a very blue sea), and like a hurricane he swept across the living room, down the length of the corridor and into the kitchen. He took a bottle of whisky from the drinks cabinet, opened the freezer and took two ice cubes which he dropped into a large tumbler, and poured himself a generous measure of the drink, then returned to the living room, all the while telling the story – shouting, laughing throughout – of how that morning he'd almost been run over. Ângela Lúcia arrived in a green dress, silently, bringing the last light with her. She stood opposite José Buchmann:

'Do you two know each other?'

'No, no!' said Ângela, her voice colourless. 'I don't think so.'

José Buchmann was even less certain:

'Oh, but there are ever so many people I don't know!' he said, and laughed at his own wit. 'I've never been all that popular.'

Ângela Lúcia didn't laugh. José Buchmann looked at her anxiously. His voice was back to that sibilant softness it had had in the early days. He told how a few days ago he'd been taking photos of a madman, one of those countless wretches who wander the city streets aimlessly, because he was fascinated by this man's particular bearing. Very early that morning he – José Buchmann – had been lying on his front in the middle of the tarmac, waiting to get a good shot of the old man as he emerged from a sewer that apparently he'd made his home, when suddenly he spotted a car lurching towards him. He rolled over to the kerb, clutching his Canon, just in time to avoid an appalling death. When he came to develop the film he discovered that in the chaos of his escape the camera had taken three shots. Two of them weren't any use. Mud. A bit of sky. But the last one clearly showed the stealthy metal of the car, and the indifferent face of the passenger sitting in the back seat. He produced the photos; Félix whistled:

'*Pópilas*! It's the President!...'

Ângela Lúcia was more interested in the piece of sky:

'That cloud, do you see? It looks like a lizard...'

José Buchmann agreed. Yes, it did look like a lizard, or perhaps a crocodile; but of course we all see whatever we want to see in the fleeting image of a cloud. When Félix returned from the kitchen, carrying in both hands a broad, deep clay bowl, the two of them had settled back down. Buchmann wanted the chilli-pepper and the lemon. He praised the consistency of the manioc-paste. Bit by bit he recovered his broad laugh and Luanda accent. Ângela Lúcia turned her soft watery eyes on him:

'Félix tells me you've spent a lot of time living abroad. Where?'

José Buchmann hesitated a moment. He turned to my friend, disquieted, in a plea for help. Félix pretended not to notice:

'Yes, yes. You've never told me where you were all those years...'

He smiled sweetly. It was as though for the first time in his life he were experiencing the pleasures of cruelty. José Buchmann sighed deeply. He leant back in his chair:

'I've spent the last ten years without any fixed home. Adrift across the world, taking photographs of wars. Before that I lived in Rio de Janeiro, and before that in Berlin, and earlier still in Lisbon. I went to Portugal in the sixties to study law, but I couldn't stand the climate. It was too quiet. *Fado*, Fátima, football... In winter – which could happen at any point in the year, and usually did – a rain of dead algae would fall from the sky. The streets would be dark with it. People died of sadness. Even the dogs hanged themselves. I fled. I went first to Paris, and from there travelled with a friend to Berlin. I washed dishes in a Greek restaurant. I worked as a receptionist in a high-class brothel. I gave the Germans Portuguese lessons. I sang in bars. I modelled for young art students. One day a friend gave me a Canon F-1, the one I still use today, and that's how I became a photographer. I was in Afghanistan in 1982, with the Soviet troops... In Salvador with the guerrillas... In Peru, on both sides... In the Falklands, again on both sides... In Iran during the war against Iraq... In Mexico on the side of the Zapatistas... I've taken a lot of photos in Israel and Palestine – a lot – there's never any shortage of work there...'

Ângela Lúcia smiled, nervous again:

'Enough! I don't want your memories to pollute this house with blood...'

Félix returned to the kitchen to prepare dessert. The two guests remained, seated opposite one another. Neither spoke. The silence that hung between them was full of murmurings, of shadows, of things that run along in the distance, in some remote time, dark and furtive. Or perhaps not. Perhaps they just remained without speaking, sitting there opposite each other, because they simply had nothing to say, and I merely imagined the rest.

Dream No. 4

I saw myself wandering along a walkway made of planks of wood laid side
by side. The walkway wound along, suspended a metre above the sand,
disappearing into the distance between the taller dunes, and then re-
emerging up ahead, sometimes completely covered by the vegetation of
the grasses and bushes, at other times totally exposed. The sea, to my right,
was smooth and luminous, turquoise blue, the sort of sea you only find in
tourist brochures and happy dreams, and there was a smell rising from it,
a hot smell of algae and salt. A man was walking towards me. Even before
I could make out his features I knew right away that it was my friend
Félix Ventura. I could tell that the sun was bothering him. He was wearing
impenetrable dark glasses, coarse linen trousers and a loose shirt – also
linen – that flapped in the breeze like a flag. His head was covered with a
lovely panama hat, but neither this nor his elegant outfit seemed enough
to save him from the torture of the sun.

'I'm a man with no colour,' he said. 'And as you know, nature abhors a
vacuum.'

We sat down on a broad and comfortable bench that had been planted
on the walkway. The sea stretched itself out serenely at our feet. Félix
Ventura took off his hat and used it to fan his face. His skin glowed pink,
covered in sweat. I felt sorry for him:

'In cold countries people with light skin aren't so troubled by the
harshness of the sun. Maybe you ought to think about moving to
Switzerland. Have you ever been to Geneva? I'd rather like to live in
Geneva.'

'My problem isn't the sun!' he retorted. 'It's the lack of melanin.' He laughed: 'Have you noticed that anything inanimate gets bleached whiter in the sun, but living things get more colour?'

Could he really lack a soul, lack life? I denied this vehemently. I've never known anyone so alive. It seemed that he had not only a life but several lives, in and around him. Félix looked at me carefully:

'Sorry to ask – but could you tell me your name?'

'I have no name,' I replied quite frankly. 'I am the gecko.'

'That's silly. No one is a gecko!'

'You're right. No one's a gecko. And you – are you really called Félix Ventura?'

My question seemed to offend him. He lay back on the bench and his eyes disappeared into the incredible depths of the sky. I was worried that he would leap into it. I didn't know the place where we were. I couldn't remember ever having been there before, in my other life. Massive cacti, some of them several metres tall, rose up between the dunes, behind us, they too dazzled by the limpid brilliance of the sea. A flock of flamingos slipped with fiery calm across the blue sky, right over our heads, and it was only then that I was totally sure that this was, in fact, a dream. Félix turned, slowly, his eyes moist:

'Is this madness?'

I didn't know how to answer him.

I, Eulálio

The following night Félix asked Ângela Lúcia the same question. First, of course, he'd told her that he'd dreamed about me again. I've seen Ângela Lúcia say very serious things laughing, or on the contrary, adopting a sombre expression when joking with her interlocutor. It's not always possible to tell what she's thinking. On this occasion she laughed at the anxiety in my friend's eyes, greatly increasing his disquiet, but then right away turned more serious and asked:

'And his name? So did the guy tell you who he is?'

No one is a name! I thought, forcefully…

'No one is a name!' Félix replied.

The reply took Ângela Lúcia by surprise. Félix too. I watched him look at her as though looking into an abyss. She was smiling sweetly. She lay her right hand on the albino's left arm. She whispered something in his ear, and he relaxed.

'No,' he whispered back. 'I don't know who he is. But since I'm the one who dreams about him I think I can give him any name I want, can't I? I'm going to call him Eulálio, because he's so well-spoken.'

Eulálio?! That seems fine to me. So Eulálio I shall be.

Rain on Childhood

It's raining. Thick drops of water, blown by the strong winds, throw themselves at the windowpanes. Félix, who's sitting facing the storm, is savouring a fruit shake in small spoonfuls. For the past few nights this has been his dinner. He makes it himself, taking a papaya, piercing it with a fork, then he gets two passion fruit, a banana, raisins, pine nuts, a soup-spoon of muesli (an English brand) and a strand of honey.

'Have I told you about the locusts?'

He had told me.

'Whenever it rains like this it reminds me of the locusts. It wasn't here, I've never seen anything like it here in Luanda. My father, old Fausto Bendito, inherited a farm in Gabela from his maternal grandmother. We used to go spend our holidays there. I felt like I was visiting Paradise. I used to play all day long with the workers' children, and one or other of the local white boys from the area, who knew how to speak *quimbundo*. We used to play cowboys and Indians, with slingshots and spears we made ourselves, and even with air rifles – I had one, and another boy had one, which we loaded up with *maças-da-India*. You probably don't know *maças-da-India*, they're a little red fruit, about the size of a bullet. They were perfect as ammunition because when they hit their target they'd disintegrate – *pluf!* – staining the victim's clothes with what looked like blood. When I see rain like this it reminds me of Gabela. Of the mango trees on the side of the road, even on the road out of Quibala. The omelettes – I've never tasted any like them! – the omelettes that they served for breakfast at the Quibala Hotel. My childhood is full of marvellous flavours. It smelled good too. Yes, I remember the locusts. I remember the afternoons when it rained locusts. The horizons would darken. The locusts would fall, stunned, into the grasses – one here, then another there, and they'd be eaten right off by the birds, and then the darkness would get closer, covering everything, and the next moment transforming itself into a nervous, multiple thing, a furious buzzing, a commotion, and we'd make for the house, running for shelter, as the trees lost their leaves and the grass disappeared, in just a few minutes, consumed by that sort of living fire. The next day everything that had been green was gone. Fausto Bendito told me he'd seen a little green car disappear like that, consumed by locusts. He was probably exaggerating.'

I like listening to him. Félix talks about his childhood as though he'd really lived through it. He closes his eyes. He smiles:

'When I close my eyes I can see those locusts again, falling from the sky. The red ants, warrior ants – you know what I mean? – red ants would come down at night, they'd come from some doorway in the night that leads to hell, and they'd multiply, to thousands, millions, as fast as we could kill them. I remember waking up coughing, coughing violently, suffocating, my eyes burning, from the smoke of battle. My father Fausto Bendito, in his pyjamas, grey hair completely dishevelled, his bare feet in a basin of water, fighting that sea of ants with a pump full of DDT. Fausto shouting instructions to the servants through the smoke. I laughed with a child's amazement. I'd fall asleep and dream of the red ants, and when I awoke they'd still be there, in the middle of all that smoke, that bitter smoke, millions of those little grinding machines, with their blind fury and their ancestral hunger. I'd fall asleep, and dream, and they'd make their way into my dreams, I'd see them climbing the walls, I'd see them attacking the chickens in their coop, the doves in the dovecote. The dogs would bite at their paws. They'd run in circles, spinning in rage, they'd run in circles howling, their teeth trying to snatch the red ants that were clinging to their toes, they'd run, they'd howl, they'd bite themselves. They'd bite off the red ants, and their toes with them. The patio would be covered in blood. And the smell of blood maddened the dogs even more. It maddened the red ants. Old Esperança – who wasn't all that old in those days – would shout, beg, *Do something, master! The animals are suffering!* and I remember my father loading the hunting rifle, while she dragged me into my room so I wouldn't watch... Esperança would hold me, my face buried in her breasts, but it was no use. When I close my eyes now, I can still see them. I can hear it all – would you believe it? Even today I cry over the deaths of my dogs. I shouldn't say this, really – I'm not sure you'll understand me – but I mourn the death of my dogs more than my poor father. We awoke, shook down our hair, our sheets, and the red ants would drop out dead, or almost dead, but still biting randomly, chewing at the air with their thick iron pincers. It rained, fortunately. The rain came through the illuminated sky and we'd go running – bounding – out to that thick, clean water, drinking in the perfume of the wet earth. And the first rains brought the white ants with them. All night long they'd spin about the lights like a mist, with a sweet humming, until they lost their wings, and in the morning we'd find the path carpeted with them, fine and transparent. I've always thought of white ants and butterflies as creatures quite without malice. In olden days stories for children always used to end with the words, *and they lived happily ever after*, this being after the Prince has married the Princess and they've had lots of children. In life there's never a plot that works out like that, of course. Princesses marry bodyguards, they marry trapeze-artists and life goes on, and they live unhappily until they separate. And years later, just like the rest of us, they die. We're only happy – truly happy – when it's for ever-after, but only children live in a world where things can last forever. I was happy ever after in my childhood, there in Gabela, in the long holidays, as I tried to build a fort in the branches of an acacia tree. I was happy ever after on the banks of a brook, a strip of running water so modest that it didn't even bother with the luxury of a name, but proud enough for us to think it more than a mere brook – it was the River. It ran through plantations of corn and manioc, and that's where we'd go to catch tadpoles, to sail improvised steamboats, and also, as evening drew in, to spy on the washerwomen while they bathed. I was happy with my dog, *Cabiri*, the two of us were happy ever after, chasing pigeons and rabbits through the long afternoons, playing hide-and-seek in the tall grasses. I was happy on the deck of *Príncipe Perfeito*, on an endless journey from Luanda to Lisbon, throwing bottles with innocent messages into the sea. *Whoever finds this bottle, please write to me.* No one ever wrote to me. In catechism lessons an old priest with a faint voice and a weary gaze tried to explain to me what Eternity was. For me it seemed like just another name for my summer holidays. The priest talked of angels, and I saw chickens. To this day, in fact, of all the things I've seen, chickens are still the ones that most closely resemble angels. He talked of heavenly joy, and I saw chickens scrabbling away in the sun, digging up little nests in the sand, turning their little glass eyes in pure mystical bliss. I can't imagine Paradise without chickens. I can't even imagine the Great God, reclining lazily on a fluffy bed of clouds, without his being surrounded by a gentle host of chickens. You know something – I've never known a bad chicken – have you? Chickens, like white ants, like butterflies, are altogether immune against evil.'

The rain redoubled its strength. Rain like this is unusual in Luanda. Félix Ventura wipes his face with a handkerchief. He still uses cotton handkerchiefs, massive things, with old-style patterns on them, and his name embroidered into one corner. I envy him his childhood. Maybe it's not real. But I envy him it all the same.

Between Life and Books

As a child, before I'd even learned to read, I used to spend long hours in the library of our house, sitting on the floor, leafing through big illustrated encyclopaedias, while my father composed arduous verses that later – very sensibly – he would destroy. Later, when I was at school, I'd hide myself away in libraries to avoid playing the always too rough games with which boys of my own age used to occupy themselves. I was a shy boy, skinny, an easy target for other boys' mockery. I grew – I grew a bit more than most, actually – my body developed, but I remained withdrawn, shy of adventure. I worked for years as a librarian, and I think I was happy in those days. I've been happy since, even now, in this little body to which I'm condemned, as through some mediocre romance or other I follow other people's happiness from a distance. Happy love affairs are unusual in great literature. And yes, I do still read books. As night falls I scan their spines. At night I entertain myself with the books that Félix has left open, forgotten on his bedside table. For some reason – I'm not sure why – I miss the *Thousand and One Nights*, the English version by Richard Burton. I must have been eight or nine when I read it for the first time, hidden from my father, since in those days it was considered obscene. I can't go back to the *Thousand and One Nights*, but to compensate I am discovering new writers. I do like the Boer writer Coetzee, for instance, for his harshness and precision, the despair totally free of self-indulgence. I was surprised to discover that the Swedes recognised such good writing.

I remember a narrow yard, a well, a turtle asleep in the mud. A bustle of people were walking on the other side of the fence. I still remember the houses, set low in the fine, sandy light of dusk. My mother was always beside me – a fragile and ferocious woman – teaching me to fear the world and its countless dangers.

'Reality is painful and imperfect,' she'd say. 'That's just the way it is, that's how we distinguish it from dreams. When something seems absolutely lovely we think it can only be a dream, and we pinch ourselves just to be sure we're really not dreaming – if it hurts it's because we're not dreaming. Reality can hurt us, even those moments when it may seem to us to be a dream. You can find everything that exists in the world in books – sometimes in truer colours, and without the real pain of everything that really does exist. Given a choice between life and books, my son, you must choose books!'

My mother! From now on I'll just call her *Mother*.

Imagine a young man racing along on his motorcycle, on a minor road. The wind is beating at his face. The young man closes his eyes, and opens his arms wide, just like they do in films, feeling himself completely alive and in communion with the universe. He doesn't see the lorry lunging out from the crossing. He dies happy. Happiness is almost always irresponsible. We're happy for those brief moments when we close our eyes.

The Small World

José Buchmann laid the photographs out on the big living room table, large A4 copies, black and white on matt paper. Almost all of them showed the same man: an old man, tall, slender, with a mass of white hair that tumbled down to his chest in thick plaits then disappeared into the heavy strands of his beard. As he appeared in the photographs – dressed in a dark shirt, in tatters, on which you could still make out a sickle and hammer on his chest, and with his head held high, his eyes ablaze with fury – he'd remind you of some olden-day prince now fallen into disgrace.

'I've followed him everywhere these past few weeks, morning to night. Want to see? Let me show you the city from the perspective of a wretched dog.'

a) The old man, seen from behind, walking along disembowelled streets.

b) Ruined buildings, their walls pockmarked with bullet-holes, thin bones exposed. A poster on one of the walls, announcing a concert by Julio Iglesias.

c) Boys playing football, tall buildings all around them. They're terribly thin, almost translucent. They're immersed, suspended in the dust like dancers on a stage. The old man is sitting on a rock, watching them. He's smiling.

d) The old man is sleeping in the shade of the husk of a military tank that's eaten away by rust.

e) The old man is standing up against a statue of the President, urinating.

f) The old man, swallowed up by the ground.

g) The old man emerges from the sewer like an ungovernable God, the unkempt hair glowing in the soft morning light.

'I've sold this story to an American magazine. I'm off to New York tomorrow. I'll be there a week or two. Longer, perhaps. And you know what I'm planning to do there?'

Félix Ventura wasn't expecting the answer. He shook his head.

'But that's crazy! You do realise how ridiculous that is, don't you?'

José Buchmann laughed. A serene laugh. Maybe he was just joking:

'A long time ago, when I was in Berlin, I was surprised to receive a telephone call from an old friend of mine, an old schoolmate from my beloved Chibia. He told me that two days earlier he'd left Lubango, he'd travelled by motorcycle to Luanda, and from Luanda flown to Lisbon, and then from Lisbon he'd set off for Germany – he was fleeing from the war. He had a cousin who was meant to be meeting him, but there was no one there, and so he decided to try and find his cousin's house – he left the airport, and got lost. He was anxious. He didn't speak a word of English – still less of German – and he'd never been in a big city before. I tried to calm him down. *Where are you calling from?* I asked. *From a phone box*, he replied. *I found your number in my address book and decided to call.* I agreed: *You did the right thing. Stay where you are. Just tell me what you can see around you, tell me anything you can see that looks unusual, that attracts your attention, so I can get a sense of where you are. Anything strange?* I asked. *Well, on the other side of the road there's a machine with a light that goes on and off, and changes colour, green, red, green, and in it there's a picture of a little man walking.*'

He told the whole story imitating his friend's voice, the broad accent, the anxiety of the unfortunate man on the other end of the line. He laughed again – uproariously this time – till he had tears in his eyes. He asked Félix for a glass of water. As he drank he began to calm down:

'Yes, old man, I know New York is a very big city. But if I was able to find a traffic light in Berlin, and a phone box opposite it, with an *acorrentado* – a man in chains... that's what they call people from Chibia, did you know that?... If I was able to find a phone box in Berlin with an *acorrentado* inside it, waiting for me, I should in New York be able to find a decorator called Eva Miller – my mother! God, my mother! Within the fortnight I'm sure I'll find her.'

My dear friend,

I do hope this letter finds you in excellent health. I realise that what I'm writing you isn't really a letter, but an email. No one writes letters any more these days. But to tell you the truth, I do miss those days when people communicated by exchanging letters – real letters, on good paper, to which you might add a drop of perfume, or attach dried flowers, coloured feathers, a lock of hair. I feel a flicker of nostalgia for those days, when the postman used to bring our letters to the house, and we were glad, surprised to see what we'd received, what we opened and read, and at the care we took when we replied, choosing each word, weighing it up, assessing its light, feeling its fragrance, because we knew that every word would later be weighed up, studied, smelled, tasted, and that some might even escape the maelstrom of time, to be re-read many years later. I can't stand the rude informality of emails. I always feel horror, physical horror, metaphysical and moral horror, when I see that 'Hi!' – how can we possibly take seriously anyone who addresses us like that? Those European travellers who spent the nineteenth century travelling across the backwoods of Africa always used to refer jokingly to the elaborate greetings exchanged by the native guides when – during the course of a long journey – they happened to cross paths with a friend or relative in some favourably shady spot. The white man would wait impatiently, until after several long minutes of laughter, interjections and clapping had passed, he finally interrupted the guide:

'So what did the men say? Have they seen Livingstone or not?'

'Oh, no, they haven't said anything about that, boss,' the guide explained. 'They were just saying hello.'

I expect just that time-span from a letter. Let us pretend that this is a letter, and that the postman has just handed it to you. Perhaps it would smell of the fear that nowadays people sweat and breathe in this vast, rotting apple. The sky here is dark, and low. I keep making wishes that clouds like these might float over to Luanda, a perpetual mist which would suit your sensitive skin; and wishes too that your business carries on, full steam ahead. I'm sure it must do, as we all so need a good past, especially those people who misgovern us in our sad country, as they govern it.

I always think of the lovely Ângela Lúcia (I do think she is beautiful) as I beat my way rather disheartened through the anxious chaos of these streets. Perhaps she's right, perhaps the important thing is to bear witness not to the darkness (as I've always done) but to the light. If you're with our friend do tell her that she did manage at least to sow the seeds of doubt in me, and that in the past few days I've lifted my eyes up to the sky more often than ever before in my life. By lifting our gaze we don't see the mud, we don't see the little creatures scrabbling in it. So what do you think, Félix – is it more important to bear witness to beauty, or to denounce horror?

Maybe my careless philosophising is beginning to annoy you. If you've read this far I imagine you're beginning to understand what it was like being one of those European travellers I referred to earlier:

'So what does this guy want? Did he find Livingstone or didn't he?'

No, I didn't. By consulting the telephone directories I was able to find six Millers called 'Eva', but none had been in Angola. I then decided to put an ad in Portuguese in five popular newspapers. Not one response. But then I did find my way onto the trail... I don't know if you're familiar with the Small World Theory, also known as Six Degrees of Separation. In 1967 the American sociologist Stanley Milgram of Harvard University set up an odd challenge for three hundred residents of Kansas and Nebraska. His hope was that these people – using only information obtained from friends and acquaintances by letter (this being in the days when people still exchanged letters) – would be able to make contact with two people in Boston, for whom they knew only their name and profession. Sixty people agreed to take part in the challenge. Three succeeded. When he came to analyse the results, Milgram realised that there were on average just six contacts between the originator and the target. If his theory was correct, I'm now just two people away from my mother. Everywhere I go I bring with me a cutting from the U.S. edition of Vogue, the one you gave me, which reproduced an Eva Miller watercolour. The report was signed by a journalist by the name of Maria Duncan. She left the magazine years ago, but the Editor still remembered her. After a lot of hunting around I was able to track down a telephone number for her in Miami, where Maria lived when she still worked for Vogue. My call was answered by a nephew of hers, who told me his aunt no longer lived there. After the death of her husband she'd gone back to the city of her birth, New York. She gave me the address. And would you believe the irony? – it's a block from the hotel where I was staying. I went to see her yesterday. Maria Duncan is an elderly lady with scrawny gestures, purple hair, and a strong, certain voice that seems to have been stolen from a much younger woman. I suspect that loneliness weighs heavily on her – it's an ill that befalls old people, and so common in big cities. She welcomed me with some interest, and when she learned of the reason for my visit became even more excited. A son looking for his mother – bound to touch any feminine heart. 'Eva Miller?' – no, the name didn't mean anything to her. I showed her the cutting from Vogue and she went off to fetch a box of old photographs, magazines and cassettes, and the two of us spent hours rummaging through it all, like two children in their grandparents' attic. It paid off. We found a photo of her with my mother. And more importantly, we found a letter that Eva had written to her to thank her for sending the copy of the magazine. The envelope bore an address in Cape Town. I imagine Eva had been based in Cape Town before settling in New York. But I fear that in order to find her here — or wherever she now is — I'll have to retread her whole tortured path. I fly to Johannesburg tomorrow, on my way back to Luanda; it's just a step or two from Johannesburg to Cape Town. It may be a most important step for me. Wish me luck, and receive an affectionate greeting from your true friend,

   José Buchmann

The Scorpion

Out of habit, and out of genetic predisposition (because bright light bothers me), I sleep during the day, all day. Sometimes, however, something will wake me up – a noise, a ray of sunlight – and I'm forced to make my way across the discomfort of the daytime, running along walls till I find a deeper crack, a deeper damper crack where I can, once again, rest. I don't know what it was that woke me this morning. I think I was dreaming about something severe (I can never remember faces, only feelings). Perhaps I was dreaming about my father. The moment I awoke I saw the scorpion. He was just a few centimetres away. Motionless. Closed in a shell of hatred like a mediaeval warrior in his armour. And then he fell upon me. I jumped back, climbed the wall, in a flash, until I was up at the ceiling. I could hear quite clearly the dry tap of the sting against the floor – I can hear it still.

I remember something my father said once when we were celebrating – with only pretend joy, I like to think – the death of someone we disliked:

'He was evil, and he didn't know it. He didn't know what evil was. That is to say, he was *pure* evil.'

That's what I felt at precisely the moment that I opened my eyes and the scorpion was there.

The Minister

After the episode with the scorpion I wasn't able to get back to sleep. This meant that I was able to witness the arrival of the Minister. A short, fat man, ill at ease in his body. To watch him you'd think he'd been shortened only moments earlier and hadn't yet become accustomed to his new height... He was wearing a dark suit, with white stripes, which didn't really fit and which troubled him. He lowered himself with a sigh of relief into the wicker chair, with his fingers wiped the thick sweat on his face, and before Félix had the chance to offer him a drink he shouted to Old Esperança:

'A beer, woman! Nice and cold!'

My friend raised an eyebrow, but restrained himself. Old Esperança brought the beer. Outside, the sun was melting the tarmac.

'So you don't have air conditioning in this place then?!'

This he said with horror. He drank up the beer in large gulps, greedily, and asked for another. Félix told him to make himself at home – wouldn't he like to take off his jacket, perhaps? The Minister accepted. In his shirtsleeves he looked even fatter, even shorter, as though God had carelessly sat down on his head.

'Do you have anything against air conditioning?' he joked. 'Does it offend your principles?...'

This sudden camaraderie irritated my friend even more. He coughed, a bark of a cough, then went off to fetch the file he'd prepared. He opened it on the little mahogany table – slowly, theatrically – in a ritual I'd observed so many times. It always worked. The Minister, anxious, held his breath as my friend revealed his genealogy to him:

'This is your paternal grandfather, Alexandre Torres dos Santos Correia de
Sá e Benevides, a direct descendent of Salvador Correia de Sá e Benevides,
the famous *carioca* who in 1648 liberated Luanda from the Dutch...'

'Salvador Correia?! The fellow they named the high school after?'

'That's the one.'

'I thought he was Portuguese! Or a politician from the capital, or some
colonial; otherwise why did they change the name of the school to Mutu
Ya Kevela?'

'I suppose it was because they wanted an Angolan hero – in those days
we needed our own heroes like we needed bread to feed us. Though, if
you'd rather I can fix up another grandfather for you. I could arrange
documents to show that you're descended from Mutu ya Kevela himself,
or N'Gola Quiluange, or even Queen Ginga herself. Would you rather
that?'

'No, no, I'll keep the Brazilian. Was the fellow rich?'

'Extremely. He was cousin to Estácio de Sá, founder of Rio de Janeiro,
who – poor man – met a sad end, when the Tamoio Indians caught him
with a poisoned arrow full in the face. But anyway, what you will want to
know is that during the years he spent here, running this city of ours,
Salvador Correia met an Angolan woman – Estefânia – the daughter of
one of the most prosperous slave-traders of the day, Felipe Pereira Torres
dos Santos, and fell in love with her. And from that love – an illicit love I
hasten to add, as the governor was a married man – from that love three
sons were born. I've got the family tree here, look – it's a work of art.'

The Minister was astonished:

'Fantastic!'

And indignant:

'Damn! Whose stupid idea was it to change the name of the high
school?! A man who expelled the Dutch colonists, an internationalist
fighter of our brother-country, an Afro-antecedent, who gave us one of
the most important families in this country – that is to say, mine. No, old
man, it won't do. Justice must be restored. I want the high school to go
back to being called Salvador Correia, and I'll fight for it with all my
strength. I'll have a statue of my grandfather cast to put outside the
entrance. A really big statue, in bronze, on a block of white marble. (Yes,
marble – don't you think?) Salvador Correia, on horseback, treading with
contempt on the Dutch colonisers... The sword's important. I'll buy a real

sword – he did use a sword, didn't he? Yes, a real sword, bigger than the one Afonso Henriques has got. And you can write something for the gravestone. Something along the lines of *Salvador Correia, Liberator of Angola with the gratitude of the nation and the Marimba Union Bakeries* – something like that, or something else, whatever, but something respectful – yes, hell, respectful! Have a think about it and get back to me. Oh and look, I've brought you some sweets, *ovos moles* from Aveiro – do you like *ovos moles*? These are the best *ovos moles* in Aveiro, though in fact they're "Made in Cacuaco", the best *ovos moles* in all Africa, in the whole world – even better than the real thing. Made by my master-patissier, who's from Ilhavo – do you know Ilhavo? You ought to. You people spend two days in Lisbon and think you know Portugal. But try them, try them, then tell me if I'm right or not. So I'm descended from Salvador Correia – *caramba*! – and I never knew it till now. Excellent. My wife will be ever so pleased.'

The Fruit of Difficult Years

Ângela Lúcia arrived just a few minutes after the Minister had said his goodbyes. The heat didn't appear to bother her at all. She came in clean and composed, her braids reflecting light, with a fresh pomegranate glow to her tanned skin. A delight, in other words:

'Am I bothering you?'

There was nothing in the question, or in the smile that accompanied it, to suggest that she would have minded if she were. It was, rather, a challenge. My friend kissed her cheek, shyly. A single kiss.

'You're never any trouble...'

She hugged him.

'You're so lovely.'

Later, after the night had drawn in, Félix made a confession:

'One of these days I'm going to lose my head and kiss you on the lips...'

He wanted to grab her arms and push her up against the wall, as though she were one of those girls he brings home every once in a while. It would be difficult. I'd swear that Ângela Lúcia's fragility is nothing but a ruse. This evening she switched roles, from dove to serpent, in the blink of an eye:

'Your grandfather, him over there, in the picture, he looks a lot like Frederick Douglass.'

Félix looked at her, defeated:

'Ah, so you recognised him? Well, what do you expect? That's called professional distortion. I create plots for a living. I fabricate so much, all day long, and so enthusiastically, that sometimes I reach night-time so lost in the labyrinth of my own fantasies... Yes, that's Frederick Douglass. I bought him in a street market in New York. But the person who brought over the big chair you're sitting in was in fact one of my great-grandfathers, or rather, the grandfather of my adopted father. Apart from the bit about the portrait, everything I've told you about my background is quite true. Or at least, as much of it as I remember. I know I have false memories sometimes – we all do, don't we?... there have been studies done by psychologists of this – but I think this much is true.'

'I can believe it. But your friend José Buchmann, that story is completely made-up, isn't it? You invented him yourself...'

Félix denied it vehemently. No, damn it! If it had been anyone else suggesting it he might have been offended – very offended, even – but thinking about it, it was in a way a sort of compliment, as no one but Reality could possibly have come up with someone as unrealistic as José Buchmann:

'If you ask me, whenever I hear about something completely impossible I believe it at once. And don't you think José Buchmann is impossible? Yes, we both do. So he has to be for real.'

Ângela Lúcia enjoyed the paradox, and laughed. Félix made the most of the moment to make his escape:

'Talking about family histories, you know you've never told me yours? I know almost nothing about you...'

She shrugged her shoulders. Her whole life story, she said, could be summed up in just five lines. She was born in Luanda. She grew up in Luanda. One day she decided to leave the country and travel. She travelled a lot, taking photographs wherever she went, and in time she returned. She'd like to keep travelling, keep taking photographs – it's what she knows how to do. There was nothing interesting in her life, save for the two or three interesting people she'd met along the way. Félix insisted. So was she an only child, or had she grown up surrounded by brothers and sisters? And her parents, what did they do? Ângela made a gesture of annoyance. She stood up. Then she sat down again. She'd been an only child for four years. Then came two sisters and a brother. Their father was an architect, their mother an airline stewardess. Her father wasn't an alcoholic, he didn't even drink, and no, she hadn't ever been sexually abused by him. Her parents loved each other; every Sunday he would give her flowers; every Sunday in exchange she would give him a poem. Even in the difficult years – she'd been born in seventy-seven, a child of that difficult time – they'd never lacked for anything. She'd had a simple, happy childhood. Which was to say, her life would never make much of a novel – still less a modern novel. You couldn't write a novel these days, even a short story, without the female lead being raped by an alcoholic father. Her only talent as a child, she went on, had been to draw rainbows. She spent her whole childhood drawing rainbows. One day, when she turned twelve, her father gave her a camera, a basic plastic thing, and she stopped drawing them. She began to take photographs of rainbows. She sighed…

'… to this day.'

Félix had met Ângela Lúcia at the launch of an exhibition of paintings. I think – but this is just supposition on my part – that he fell in love with her the moment they exchanged their first words, as his whole life had prepared him to give himself to the first woman who upon seeing him didn't recoil in horror. When I say 'recoil', you must understand that I don't mean this literally. When introduced to Félix Ventura there are, of course, women who do literally recoil, who take a step back while offering their hand; the majority of women, however, recoil in spirit – which is to say, they offer him their hand (or cheek), saying 'A pleasure', then avert their eyes and make some flimsy comment about the state of the weather. Ângela Lúcia had offered him her cheek, he'd kissed her, she'd kissed him back, then she'd said:

'You know, that's the first time I've kissed an albino.'

When Félix explained to her what he did for a living – 'I'm a genealogist' – which is what he always says when he meets strangers – she became interested at once.

'Seriously? You're the first genealogist I've met.'

They had left the exhibition together, and went to continue their conversation on the terrace of a bar, under the stars, looking out over the black waters of the bay. That night, Félix told me, only he had spoken. Ângela Lúcia possesses a rare gift, an ability to remain engaged in a conversation without hardly speaking at all. Then my friend had returned home, and said to me:

'I've met a remarkable woman. Oh, my friend, I don't have the words to describe her – everything about her is Light.'

I thought he was exaggerating. Where there is light, there are shadows too.

Dream No. 5

José Buchmann was smiling. A faint, mocking smile. We were in the luxury car of an old steam train. There was a canvas hanging on one of the walls, which lit the air with a faint copper-coloured glow. I noticed a chessboard, dark wood and marble, on a little table between us. I didn't remember having moved any of the pieces, but the game was clearly progressing. The photographer was doing rather better.

'At last,' he said, 'I've been dreaming of this for several days. I wanted to see you. I wanted to know what you were like.'

'So do you think this conversation is real?'

'The conversation, certainly; it's just the setting that is rather lacking in substance. There is truth – even if there isn't realism – in everything a man dreams. A guava tree in bloom, for instance, lost in the pages of a good novel, can bring delight with its fictional perfume to any number of real rooms.'

I was forced to agree. At times, for example, I dream that I'm flying. And I've never flown so truly, with such authority, as in my dreams. Flying on a plane – in the days when I used to fly by plane – never gave me the same feeling of freedom. I've cried in dreams over the death of my grandmother, but it was better than my waking crying. And in truth I've shed more authentic tears for the deaths of literary characters than I ever did for the disappearance of many of my friends and relatives. What seemed least real to me was that canvas on the wall behind José Buchmann, a melancholy composition, not because of its subject – it wasn't clear what its subject was, which may be the greatest virtue of modern art – but because of the glow of its colours. Through the windows, evening was drawing in, quickly. We saw beaches rush by, and trees laden with coconuts, the big uncombed mane of the *casuarina* tree. We even saw the sea, out there in the distance, burning in a massive fire of indigo blue. The train slowed to climb an incline, it panted like an asthmatic, an old mechanical beast, almost breathless. José Buchmann moved his queen forward, threatening my king's knight. I sacrificed a pawn, which he looked at, absent-mindedly.

'The truth is improbable.'

A lightning smile.

'Lies,' he explained, 'are everywhere. Even nature herself lies. What is camouflage, for instance, but a lie? The chameleon disguises itself as a leaf in order to deceive a poor butterfly. He lies to it, saying *Don't worry, my dear, can't you see I'm just a very green leaf waving in the breeze*, and then he jets out his tongue at six hundred and twenty-five centimetres a second, and eats it.'

He took my pawn. I was silent, dazed by the revelation and by the distant brilliance of the sea. I could only remember someone else's phrase:

'I hate lying, because it's inexact.'

José Buchmann recognised the words. He considered them a moment, assessing their solidity and their mechanism, their efficiency:

'Truth has a habit of being ambiguous too. If it were exact it wouldn't be human.' As he spoke he became increasingly animated. 'You quoted Ricardo Reis. Allow me, then, to quote Montaigne: *Nothing seems true that cannot also seem false.* There are dozens of professions for which knowing how to lie is a virtue. I'm thinking of diplomats, statesmen, lawyers, actors, writers, chess players. I'm thinking of our common friend Félix Ventura, without whom you and I would never have met. Name a profession – any profession – that doesn't sometimes have recourse to lying, a profession in which a man who only tells the truth would be welcomed?'

I felt hemmed in. He moved a bishop. I responded, moving my knight. A few days ago I saw a basketball player on television, a naïve sort, complaining about journalists:

'Sometimes they don't write what I mean, they just write what I say.'

I told him this, and he laughed with pleasure. I was already beginning to find him less disagreeable. The train gave a long whistle, then a bewildered, long drawn-out howl, like a red ribbon stretched across the seafront. A group of fishermen on the beach waved to the train. José

Buchmann responded to their wave with a bold gesture. Just a few minutes earlier, when the train had made a brief stop, he'd leaned out of the window to buy mangoes; I heard him speaking to the fruit sellers in a tight, sing-song language which seemed to me to be composed exclusively of vowels. He told me that he spoke English – in its various accents – and a number of German dialects, Parisian French and Italian. He assured me, too, that he was able to discourse with as much self-assurance in Arabic or Romanian.

'I can also speak Groan,' he joked, 'the secret language of the camels. I speak Grunt, like a true-born wild boar. I speak Buzz, and the Chirp language of the crickets – and even the Caw of the crows. On my own in a garden I could discuss philosophy with the magnolias.'

He peeled one of the mangoes with a Swiss army knife, cut it in half, and gave me the larger piece. He ate his piece. He told me about a small island in the Pacific where he'd spent a few months, in which lying is considered the most solid pillar of society. The Ministry of Information, a revered, almost sacred institution, was charged with creating and propagating inaccurate news. Once this information is on the loose among the crowds, it grows, takes on new forms, eventually forms that contradict one another, generating copious popular movements and making society more dynamic. Let's imagine that unemployment reached levels that were considered dangerous. The Ministry of Information – or simply, The Ministry – would start circulating the story that there had been a discovery of deep-sea petroleum within the country's own territorial waters. The possibility of an imminent economic boom would revive trade, expatriate technicians would return home, keen to be a part of the reconstruction, and before long new companies and new jobs would be created. Of course, things don't always pan out as the technicians predict. There was this one time, for example, when The Ministry (who whatever their name may suggest have always been a politically independent body) launched an attack on an opponent, hoping to destroy his career, spreading a suspicion that he'd been having an extra-marital affair with an English singer. The rumour grew in size and strength, so much so that the opponent ended up divorcing his wife and marrying the singer (whom he'd never met before this had all started), earning him massive popularity and seeing him elected some years later to the Presidency.

'The impossibility of controlling rumours,' he concluded, 'is the main virtue of such a system. That's what gives the Ministry its near-divine nature. Check!'

I could see that I had lost the game. I decided to take a risk and offer him up my queen.

'Félix Ventura says that he believes in things when they seem impossible – and that's why he believes in you...'

'He said that?'

'He did. But I don't believe in you. In you or in Ângela Lúcia. Whenever two or more events stumble into each other and we don't know why, we call it chance, coincidence. But what we call chance we should perhaps call ignorance. Aren't you surprised that two photographers – a man and a woman – both of whom have lived in exile for so long, should return to the country at exactly the same time?'

'I'm not, no. After all, I'm one of those photographers. But I do think it's quite natural that you should be surprised. You see, my friend, coincidences produce amazement in just the same way, and with the same carelessness, as trees produce shade – checkmate.'

I knocked over my king (the white king), and awoke.

Real Characters

The Minister was writing a book, *The Real Life of a Fighter*, a dense volume of memoirs that he was hoping to bring out before Christmas. Though to be rather more precise, he's writing his book with a hired hand – the hand of Félix Ventura. My friend dedicated a good part of his day – and even his night – to this work. As he completed each chapter he would read it to the author-to-be, discussing some detail or other, he'd take note of the criticisms and correct whatever there was to be corrected, and so they would go on. Félix would sew fiction in with reality dextrously, minutely, in such a way that historical facts and dates were respected. In the book the Minister conversed with real people (sometimes with royal people) and it would be most convenient if these people should tomorrow believe that they had indeed traded confidences and opinions with him. Our memory feeds itself to a large extent on what other people remember of us. We remember other people's memories as though they were our own – even fictional ones.

'It's like the Castle of São Jorge in Lisbon – do you know it? It has battlements, but they're fake. António de Oliveira Salazar ordered that some crenellations be added to the castle to make it more authentic. To him there was something wrong with a castle without crenellations – there was something monstrous about it – like a camel without humps. So the fake part of the Castle of São Jorge is today what makes it realistic. Several octogenarian Lisboans I've spoken to are convinced the castle has always had crenellations. There's something rather amusing about that, isn't there? If it were authentic, no one would believe in it.'

As soon as *The Real Life of a Fighter* is published, the consistency of Angola's history will change, there will be even more History. The book will come to be used as a reference for future work on the struggle for the nation's liberation, on the troubled years that followed independence, and the broad movement of democratisation the country experienced. Let me give you some examples:

1) In the early seventies the Minister was a young man employed in the Luanda postal services. He played drums in a rock band who called themselves The Un-namables. He was more interested in women than in politics. That's the truth – or rather, the prosaic truth. In the book the Minister reveals that even at that time he was already dedicating himself to political activity, secretly (very secretly indeed) fighting against Portuguese colonialism. Driven by the bold blood of his ancestors (he makes several references to Salvador Correia de Sá e Benevides) – he created within the postal services a cell supporting the liberation movement. The group specialised in distributing pamphlets within letters aimed for colonial functionaries. Three of their number, the Minister among them, were turned in to the Portuguese political police and arrested on April 20th, 1974. It may be that the Carnation Revolution saved their lives.

2) The Minister left Angola in 1975, a few weeks before independence, and sought refuge in Lisbon. He was still more interested in women than in politics. Pursued by hunger he took out an advertisement in a popular newspaper: 'Master Marimba: cures for the evil eye, envy, ills of the soul. Guaranteed success in love and business.' It wasn't an ad so much as a prediction. Within months he was (by magic indeed) a rich man. Women by the dozen made their way to his consulting room. Most were hoping to recover their husbands' attentions, distance them from their mistresses, rebuild a failed marriage. Others just wanted someone to listen. He listened. His clients would pay, the Minister explained, according to their respective abilities. The women he cured offered him knitted cardigans to withstand the winter cold, and fresh eggs, and preserves. The wealthier ones handed him hefty cheques, they had electrical appliances delivered to him, good shoes, or designer clothes. A very beautiful blonde – the wife of a famous footballer – offered him herself. And eventually left him her car keys, the boot of the car filled with bottles

of whisky. After the first elections the Minister returned to Luanda, and with the money he'd accumulated from so many years of consoling unfortunately-married women, he set up a chain of bakeries – the Marimba Union Bakeries. That is the truth that the Minister told Félix. The story Félix had the man tell in his true History was that in 1975, disillusioned with the course of events, and because he refused to participate in a fratricidal war ('That hadn't been what we'd planned') the Minister went into exile in Portugal. Inspired by the teachings of his paternal grandfather, the wisest of men, well versed in the medicinal herbs of Angola, he founded in Lisbon a clinic dedicated to African alternative medicine. He returned to his country in 1990, once the civil war had come to an end, determined to contribute towards the reconstruction of the country. He wanted to give the people our-daily-bread. And that is exactly what he did.

3) The Minister's return also signalled the beginning of his involvement in politics. He began by buying favours from certain people in the so-called 'structures' in order to accelerate the licensing of his bakeries, and it wasn't long before he was a frequent visitor to the houses of ministers and generals. In just two years he himself was named Secretary of State for Economic Transparency and Combating Corruption. In *The Real Life of a Fighter* the Minister explains how – driven exclusively by great and serious patriotic motives – he accepted the burden of this first challenge. Today he is Minister for Bread-Making and Dairy Produce.

Anticlimax

There are people who from early on reveal a great talent for misfortune. Unhappiness pummels at them like a stoning, every other day, and they accept it with a resigned sigh. Others, meanwhile, have a peculiar propensity for happiness. Faced with an abyss the latter are attracted by its blueness, the former by its intoxication. Some people are destined to dream (some, indeed, are paid rather well to do so); some are born to work, practical and concrete and tireless; and there are others who are like a river, who flow effortlessly down from source to mouth, hardly straying from its bed. The case of José Buchmann, though, is I think more unusual: his inclination is to amazement. He likes to astonish people, and to be astonished himself:

'Once someone said to me, *you're no more than an adventurer.* They said it with disdain, as though they were spitting at me. And in fact I do think they were right. I seek out adventure, or rather, the unexpected, anything that lifts me out of boredom, in the way that others turn to alcohol or gambling. It's an addiction.'

Félix Ventura is looking at him with a deliberate expression of disbelief. He wants to ask the obvious question: *Did you find any sign of your mother?* – but he also knows that this would be giving in. Last time we dreamed he told me about a friend of his – the actor Orlando Sérgio – who when he goes out is often mistaken for the character he plays in a popular television series. People hug him, congratulate him or scold him, approving of what his character has done, or challenging it. Few know him by his real name. Some people even get annoyed when he tries to escape their sermons and reprimands by invoking his condition as an actor:

'My name is Orlando Sérgio, sir. You're confusing me with…'

'Don't try and kid me, old man, don't even try. Just listen to my advice, have a little patience – so you think I don't know who you are?'

Félix feels as though he's falling into exactly that same trap. José Buchmann arrived yesterday from South Africa. He arrived in a full Colonel Tapioca outfit, dressed all in khaki, with long shorts and a vest covered in pockets. As he talks he takes various things out of these pockets, with just the same assurance as a circus magician pulls rabbits from a top hat:

a)   A little bronze frog.

'It's lovely, don't you think? No? Don't you like frogs?! Well, my friend, I do like it. Did you know that there are a lot of cultures in which the frog is seen as a symbol of transformation, of spiritual metamorphosis, representing the passing to a higher level of consciousness. This is obviously because of the complicated processes of change that a frog undergoes, but also at least for some indigenous peoples in the Americas, because of the hallucinogenic properties of a poison secreted by certain species. This one is a *Bufo alvarius*, a frog from the Sonora desert. I bought it from an antique dealer in Cape Town. It was on display in the window, and I went in to buy it, as I've always been interested in frogs. If I hadn't been interested in frogs, if I hadn't gone into the shop, I never would have found this:

b)   A watercolour, only slightly larger than a postage stamp.

'They're gazelles in flight. Look at the movement of the grass, the gazelles suspended above the grass, it looks like a ballet. And now look at the signature, here, in this corner – can you read it? Eva Miller. And notice the date: August 15th, 1990. Amazing, isn't it?'

I could see that Félix was alarmed. He held the watercolour carefully between his fingers, as though he were afraid that the unlikelihood of the object could compromise its solidity.

'This can't be.' He shook his head. 'I don't know what it is you're trying to do. I'm amazed you could have gone so far…'

'Oh, come on! Do you really think I painted it myself? No, it happened just as I've told you. I found it on sale in an antiques shop in Cape Town, hidden away among dozens of other pictures of its kind. I spent all afternoon searching for other watercolours signed by her, but, alas, found nothing. The dealer had bought the whole batch of them from an Englishman who'd decided to leave the country soon after Nelson Mandela's victory. He'd lost trace of him.'

'So you weren't able to find out anything else about Eva Miller?'

José Buchmann didn't reply right away. From another pocket, inside his vest, he drew:

 c) A slim pile of photos.

'Look. This building is the one with the address that was on that letter that Eva Miller sent to Maria Duncan. It's in an area where the white middle-class live. Have you ever been to Cape Town? It's a funny place. Imagine a big, modern shopping centre, its halls decorated with tall palm trees. Beautiful palm trees. They're plastic, of course, but you wouldn't know it unless you touched them. Cape Town reminds me of a plastic palm tree. I tell you, it's an impressive city – so clean, so tidy. It's a fraud that it suits us to believe in. This is the fellow who lives in my mother's old apartment today. You see the scars? In the eighties he lived in Maputo. He was a big-shot in the South African Communist Party. One evening he got into his car, switched on the ignition, and boom! – a massive explosion. He lost an eye and both legs. He was rather nice, I thought. He's one of those people who, having spent his whole life fighting against apartheid, actually found it hard to adapt to the new rainbow nation. He complains that nowadays nobody defends ideals, that the people have been corrupted by the triumph of capitalism; he gets annoyed with democracy and all its liberal laws, but what he really misses most of all is the youth he's lost, his eye and his legs. He'd never heard of Eva Miller. But the landlord, here, in this photo, an old Boer, nearly a hundred years old, he had – he remembered my mother perfectly.'

I'd positioned myself directly above them at this point, hanging upside-down from the ceiling, in order that I might watch every detail. Félix lit the lamp to study the photographs. The picture of the old Boer (in black and white – as were all the photos, in fact) was excellent. He was sitting in a big, serious, dark wood chair. A delicate light slanted down on to the right half of his face, illuminating the silence inside him. In the bottom right-hand corner you could just make out – almost hidden in the shadows – the nervous silhouette of one of those minute little dogs that bourgeois women keep for company, and which I've always found extremely irritating, looking more like trained rats than dogs.

'Do you like that photograph? Me too.' José Buchmann smiled. 'The best photographs aren't the ones that manage to sum up a character, they're the ones that manage to sum up an age. In fact this old man received me with a certain amount of distrust, he didn't waste too many words on me, but to make up for it he did give me an ending to my pilgrimage. Want to see it?'

d) A cutting from the Johannesburg newspaper, *O Século*.

'You ready? I think this is what you might call an anticlimax. You tell me. Read it!'

Félix did as he was told:

'Eva Miller has died – This evening the North American painter Eva Miller died at her home in Sea Point, Cape Town. Having lived in southern Angola, and speaking our language perfectly, Mrs Miller had come to be well respected among South Africa's Portuguese community. In recent years she had divided her time between Cape Town and New York. The cause of her death remains unknown.'

Irrelevant Lives

Memory is a landscape watched from the window of a moving train. We watch the dawn light break over the acacia trees, the birds pecking at the morning, as though at a fruit. Further off we see the serenity of a river, and the trees embracing its banks. We see the cattle slowly grazing, a couple running, holding hands, children dancing around a football, the ball shining in the sun (another sun). We see the calm lakes where there are ducks swimming, rivers heavy with water where elephants quench their thirst. These things happen right before our very eyes, we know them to be real, but they're so far away we can't touch them. Some are so far, so very far away, and the train moving so fast, that we can't be sure any longer that they really did happen. Maybe we merely dreamed them? My memory is already failing me, we say, and maybe it was just the darkening of the sky. That's how I feel when I think of my old incarnation. I remember loose, incoherent facts, fragments of a vast dream. A woman at a party, at the very end of the party, in that vague intoxication of smoke and alcohol and pure metaphysical tiredness, grabbing my arm and whispering in my ear:

'You know, my life would make a good novel; not just any novel, a *great* novel...'

I think this happened more than once. I'm sure that most of those people have never read a great novel. I know now – I think I probably already knew then – that all lives are exceptional. Fernando Pessoa transformed the prosaic life story of a simple office worker into a *Book of Disquiet* that might possibly be the most interesting work in all of

Portuguese literature. When a few days ago I heard Ângela Lúcia confess the pointlessness of her life, I suddenly wanted to get to know her better. If a woman had one night taken me by the arm to tell me such a thing – *you know, there's nothing remarkable about my life, nothing at all, I'm barely here at all* – perhaps I would have fallen in love with her. Despite what some of my enemies may have suggested (supported secretly by many of my friends) I've always been interested in women. I liked women. I used to go out with one or other of my close female friends on long walks. When we said goodbye and hugged, the scent of their hair, the feeling of their firm breasts, they all excited me. But if one of them took the initiative and tried to kiss me, or suggested something even more daring than a kiss, I would remember Dagmar (Aurora, Alba, Lúcia) and I'd panic. I lived a prisoner to that terror for many long years.

Edmundo Barata dos Reis

When José Buchmann appeared tonight he was accompanied by an old man with a long white beard and wild braids, grey and dishevelled, cascading over his shoulders. I recognised him at once as the old tramp the photographer had been pursuing, for weeks on end, showing him – in that extraordinary image – emerging from a sewer. An ancient, vengeful God, wild-haired, with suddenly lit-up eyes.

'I'd like to introduce you to my friend Edmundo Barata dos Reis, an ex-agent of the Ministry of State Security.'

'Not ex-agent, say rather 'ex-*gent*'! Ex-exemplary citizen. Exponent of the excluded, existential excrement, an exiguous and explosive excrescence. In a word, a professional layabout. Very pleased to meet you.'

Félix Ventura offered his fingertips to the old man. He was perplexed, annoyed. Edmundo Barata dos Reis took his hand firmly in his own hands, and held it, looking at him sidelong, like a bird, attentive, mocking, enjoying the other man's discomfort. José Buchmann, wearing a lovely honey-coloured corduroy jacket, arms folded across his chest, seemed to be enjoying himself too. His little round eyes glowed in the dark of the room like shards of glass.

'I thought you'd enjoy meeting him. This man's life story could almost have been made up by you...'

'I beg your pardon?'

'I'm-All-Ears. That's what they used to call me. It was my fighting name. I liked it. I liked hearing it. And then – in a flash! – the Berlin wall collapsed on top of us. *Pópilas*, old man! Agent one day, ex-gent – ex-person – the next.'

Félix Ventura twitched:

'Did you study with Professor Gaspar?'

Edmundo Barata dos Reis smiled, surprised:

'Yes, oh yes! You too, comrade?'

With genuine joy the two men embraced. They exchanged recollections. Barata dos Reis, a good couple of years older than Félix Ventura, had been to Professor Gaspar's classes at a time when you could count the number of black students at the Liceu Salvador Correia on the fingers of one hand. Leaving school he got a job with the meteorological service. Arrested in the early sixties, accused of trying to establish a bomb-making network in Luanda, he spent seven years in the Tarrafal concentration camp in Cape Verde. 'No better than a chicken coop,' he said, 'but the beach was lovely...' Within a few weeks of independence he was already known to friends and enemies alike (and he'd always had more of the latter than the former) as Mr I'm-All-Ears. Two years in Havana, nine months in Berlin (East Berlin), another six in Moscow; his steel tempered, he returned to the solid trenches of socialism in Africa.

'A communist! Would you believe it? I'm the very last communist south of the equator...'

That insistence would be what did it for him. Within a few months he would be changed into an ideological nuisance. An awkward sort of fellow. He wasn't ashamed of shouting 'I'm a communist!' at a time when his bosses would only murmur, in hushed tones, 'I used to be a communist...' and he'd keep yelling out – 'Yes, I'm a communist, I'm really very Marxist-Leninist!' even at a time when the official version had begun to deny the country's socialist past...

'I've seen some things, old man...'

José Buchmann sat down, legs crossed, in the big wicker chair that Félix Ventura's great-grandfather had brought from Brazil. He put his right hand deep into his inside jacket pocket, took out a silver cigarette case, opened it, slowly separated some tobacco and rolled a cigarette. A wicked smile lit up his face:

'Now tell him what you told me, Edmundo, the story about the President...'

Edmundo Barata dos Reis looked at him seriously – angrily – violently tugging at the strands of his beard. For a moment I thought he was about to get up – I was afraid he might leave. José Buchmann shrugged:

'You can say it, damn it! There's nothing to worry about. Félix here is a solid chap. He's one of us. And anyway, weren't you both students of this famous Professor Gaspar? That's got to mean something. Félix tells me it's like belonging to the same tribe or something.'

'The President has been replaced with a double.' Edmundo Barata dos Reis said this in a burst, then fell silent. His eyes flitted anxiously around the room. He had begun to look like a sparrow searching for an open window, for a bit of light, a bit of sky he could escape to. He lowered his voice: 'The old man has been replaced. They've put a double in his place, a scarecrow – I'm not sure how to put it – a fucking replica.'

'Shit!' Félix burst out laughing. I'd never heard him swear before. I'd never heard him laugh like this either, with such violence. José Buchmann was surprised. Then he joined in, the two of them laughing. The three of us, laughing. One laugh drawing on another. At last Félix settled.

'So, we have a fantasy president now?' he said, wiping away his tears with a handkerchief. 'Yes, I'd suspected as much. We have a fantasy government. A fantasy justice system. We have – in other words – a fantasy country. But do tell me, *who* has replaced the President?'

Edmundo Barata dos Reis shrunk back in his chair. He didn't remind me of a God any more, he didn't remind me of a warrior – he was a dog, humiliated. He stank. He stank of urine, of rotting fruit and leaves. He straightened himself up, and instead of replying to Félix's question he addressed himself to José Buchmann, pointing at him... 'That laugh – when I hear that laugh, old man, it's as though I'm face to face with someone else, from long ago. From another time, an old time. Don't we know each other?'

'I don't believe so.' The photographer tensed. 'I'm from Chibia. Are you from Chibia?'

'What are you talking about, old man? I'm pure Luandan!'

'Then obviously not.'

'It's true,' said Félix, 'Buchmann is from the provinces, from the deep south. He's a bush-man...'

'A bushman? The bush here is more like a garden. And your gardens here in Luanda, such as they are – well, they're really more like bushland.'

145

'Take it easy. Down with tribalism. Down with regionalism. Up with people-power. Isn't that what they used to say? All I wanted was for comrade Edmundo here to answer my question. So who was it that replaced the President with a double?'

Edmundo Barata dos Reis sighed, deeply:

'The Russians, I think. Maybe the Israelis. The arms mafia, Mossad – I don't know – maybe both.'

'Could be – it would make sense. And how did you discover this coup?'

'I know the double – I hired him! I hired others too. The old man never appeared in public himself – the doubles would always appear in his place. This one – Number Three – was always the best. He was the only one who could speak without arousing suspicions – the others kept quiet, we only used them for ceremonial functions when we just needed a body in the room. But Three was a special case, an extraordinary talent, a real actor. I watched him being trained – it took five months. He learned fast – how to move, how to approach people, the tone of voice, the protocol, the old man's life story – the whole deal. By the end he was perfect. Or nearly perfect – this guy had one problem – or I should say, *has* one problem – he's left-handed. It's like looking at the President in a mirror. That's how I noticed. Haven't you spotted that the President has become left-handed all of a sudden? No, no, you haven't noticed. No one has.'

'When did you find out?'

'A year ago, a little over a year ago.'

'Were you still working for the security services then?'

'What, me?! No, old man, I've been living the life of a tramp for more than seven years now. See this shirt I'm wearing? It's become like a skin to me. It's a shirt from the Communist Party of the U.S.S.R. I put it on the day they fired me, and I've never taken it off since. I swore I wouldn't take it off until Russia went back to being communist. And now I wouldn't be able to take it off even if I wanted to. Like a skin to me – you see? I've got a hammer and sickle tattooed on my chest now. That won't come off.'

It really wouldn't come off. Félix Ventura looked at him, dazed. José Buchmann smiled, as if to say 'Well, isn't he something?' Edmundo Barata dos Reis resumed the posture of an old warrior. He shook his tough grey locks, roughly, spreading a revolting smell around him.

'Soup?' he asked. 'Don't you have any soup?'

'He's crazy!' Félix Ventura said certainly, after Edmundo Barata dos Reis had left. He said it, then said it again, firmly. He had no intention of wasting any more time on the matter. But José Buchmann insisted.

'I've heard stranger things…'

'Listen, the man's completely barking. He's flipped. You've been abroad for a long time, you don't know what's happened in this damned country. Luanda is full of people who seem completely lucid but suddenly burst out speaking impossible languages, or crying for no apparent reason, or laughing, or cursing. Some do all these things at once. Some are convinced that they're dead. There are others who really are dead, but no one's had the guts to tell them. Some think they can fly. Others believe this so strongly that they really can. It's a fairground of lunatics, this city – out there in those ruined streets, in those clusters of *musseque* houses all around town, there are pathologies that haven't even been recorded. Don't take anything they tell you too seriously. Actually, let me give you a piece of advice – don't take *anybody* seriously.'

'Maybe he isn't crazy. Maybe he's just pretending to be crazy.'

'I don't see the difference. Someone who's chosen to live on the streets, in the sewer, who believes that Russia will go back to communism, and who – on top of all that – wants people to think he's crazy… That is crazy, in my book.'

'Maybe. Maybe not.' José Buchmann seemed disheartened. 'I'd like to get to know him better.'

Love, a Crime

'We spent some tough years here.'

Félix sighed. The heat was stifling. Humidity clung to the walls. But he was sitting in the big wicker chair, sitting up straight, in a well-cut dark blue suit which drew attention to the shine of his skin. In front of him, nestling in a silk cushion, with a flower-patterned shirt and short red shorts, sat Ângela Lúcia, listening to him, smiling.

'There was a time when I used to have to do everything for myself, as I couldn't afford to pay a servant. I'd clean the house, wash clothes, cook, take care of the plants. And there wasn't any water either, so I'd have to go and fetch it, with a metal can on my head like a grocer's wife, from a hole someone had made in the tarmac – at the end of the road, at the bend by the cemetery. I was able to bear it all, for all those years, because I had Ventura. I used to shout, *Ventura, go do the washing up!* and Ventura would go. Or, *Ventura, go fetch more water!* and Ventura would go.'

'Ventura?!'

'Ventura – me. He was my double. At some point in our lives we all resort to a double.'

Ângela Lúcia liked Edmundo Barata dos Reis's theory. She loved the idea of doubles. Together they watched several tapes showing the President. I think I've already told you Félix has hundreds of videotapes. They found, to their surprise, that in the older ones the old man signed documents with his right hand. Recently he'd used only his left. Ângela Lúcia also noticed that in some shots he had a small mole beneath his left eye, and not in others.

'He may have had it removed,' Félix pointed out. 'Nowadays people get rid of all sorts of physical signs, as easily as you might wash off an ink-stain.'

Ângela was the one who noticed that the President with the mole appeared in earlier recordings, but also in ones that came later than those with the mole-less President.

'It has to have been one of the doubles!'

They played that game all afternoon. After five hours, by which time night had closed in, they'd managed to identify at least three doubles – the one with the mole, one with a slight bald patch, and a third who – Ângela swore – had a calm sea-glow in his eyes.

'I'm not going to argue with you on the subject of light,' said Félix. That's when he remembered the business with his double, Ventura: 'Believe me. We spent some tough times here.'

The woman wanted to know how he'd managed to survive during that time. Félix shrugged. He lived badly, he muttered; at first he used to rent out novels – Eça, Camilo, Jorge Amado – at a time when few people had the money to buy their own. Later on he started sending parcels of books out to Lisbon, and his father would sell them to second-hand book dealers or selected clients. Fausto Bendito Ventura had managed to buy up excellent libraries on the cheap from despairing colonials in the turbulent months leading up to independence. He'd exchange a silver ring for a bound collection of nineteenth-century Angolan newspapers. A medical library in good condition – more than a hundred volumes – cost him no more than a single silk tie, and for six dollars he acquired fifteen cases filled with history books. Years later some of the old colonials would end up buying the books back from him – in packets of ten – at their true price.

'It ended up being a good business.'

Heat was rising from the floor. It slipped in, a damp breath, through the cracks in the doors, in slow waves, carrying with it the salty smell of the sea and its murmur too, the wonder of the fish, the dim light of the moon. Ângela Lúcia's skin shone. Her shirt, clinging to her breasts. Félix still had his jacket on – he must have been baking. All I wanted was a cool crack to dive in to. I went to the kitchen – up there, through the highest windowpane, I could see over the wall of the yard to the luminous clamour of the *musseques*, and beyond them a broad black abyss, and the stars. The black abyss was the sea. I spent some time just looking out. I imagined myself sinking into that silence, blindly, like I used to, my heart leaping, my hands opening the water, at my feet a pleasant coldness, rising up my legs to my waist. I felt refreshed. When I came back to the living room I saw that Félix had taken off his jacket and was now sitting on the big cushions in front of the television, with his arms around Ângela. The ceiling-fan pushed around the warm air, the blades sweeping it lazily towards the walls. Centuries of dust, mites, old writers' souls, came away from the books and danced in the air like a mist, like a faint dream, lit by flashes from the television screen. Soundless images in black and white of the President presiding over a meeting. The President raising his fist. The President in a kit playing football. The President greeting other presidents. And then images in colour, of the President opening a park. 'The Chaves Ex-Heroes Park', read the plaque. Ângela laughed. Félix laughed. The President cut the ribbon. Félix turned back to Ângela, and kissed her on the lips. I saw her – with some surprise – closing her eyes and accepting his kiss. I heard her moan. The albino tried to undo her shirt, but she stopped him.

'No. Not that. Don't do that.'

She raised her legs elegantly, and slipped off her shorts. Through the shirt that clung to her body you could make out the roundness of her breasts, her smooth belly. Then she turned her body, till she was kneeling over Félix. Her broad shoulders – lovely swimmers' shoulders – made her waist look even slimmer. My friend sighed:

'You're so beautiful…'

Ângela took his head in her hands and kissed him. A long kiss.

It took my breath away.

Mother was little older than I, and of course as we both aged – alongside one another – the difference got smaller and smaller. Besides which I actually think she aged more slowly than I did. From a certain moment when we went out together people began to talk to me about her as 'your wife'. Maybe if she'd lived longer people would have started taking her for my daughter. I think these little mistakes used to make her happy. She insisted on calling me her 'boy'. Until the day she decided to die – nearly a hundred years old – she held the threads of my life in her hands.

'My boy mustn't come home too late.'

And I – aged eighty-something – would be terrified of coming home after midnight. If I went out with a woman friend, I felt I'd have to phone home every half hour, so Mother wouldn't torment herself. She'd be up waiting for me, vigilant, with her cat on her lap.

'My boy mustn't drink alcohol.'

And I'd sit at bar tables and drink a glass of milk, while my friends teased me affectionately and got themselves drunk on whisky or beer. And Mother went to trouble to keep me away from any women she suspected might one day take me away from Her. And she'd push the ones who were decidedly ugly – and especially the more stupid ones – into my arms, sure that I'd spurn them; and then she'd reprimand me:

'My boy plays very hard-to-get. He's going to end up on his own.'

I'm not telling you this to justify myself. It wouldn't be fair to blame Mother's zeal or my poor father's severity for my misogyny. I was who I was because I lacked the courage to be any different. I watch Félix Ventura run his fingers across the trembling body of his love, I watch him whisper sweet words in her ear, I watch him carry her to the bedroom (the woman protests, gesticulates, cries out laughing happily) and lay her down on the bed. And I watch him – at last – fall asleep, exhausted – and I begin to understand how I have come to be here.

Félix sleeps, his right arm across Ângela's chest, his hand resting on her breast. Her eyes are open. She's smiling. Carefully she disentangles herself and gets up. She puts on her flowered t-shirt, nothing else. She has long, smooth legs, incredibly thin at her ankles. She crosses the room without a sound. Keeping the darkness away with her fingertips, she opens the bathroom door, switches on the light and goes in. She takes off the t-shirt. She washes her face, her shoulders, her armpits. I notice a group of dark, round scars on her back, which stick out like insults on her golden velvet skin. I think I can see – in the mirror – just the same marks on her breasts and stomach. I go back to the bedroom, Félix is murmuring something. I think I catch the word 'savannah'. I'd like to talk to him. Perhaps if I were to sleep now I'd find him in his white suit, in coarse linen, and his beautiful panama hat, sitting under a tall baobab tree, somewhere in that savannah he's crossing in his dreams.

Ding ding!

The doorbell. *Ding ding!* An urgent ringing. Knocking. *Ding ding!* Félix leaps out of bed, white and naked as a ghost, reaches for the lamp on the bedside table and turns it on. Ângela Lúcia appears beside him, alarmed, a towel around her body:

'Who was it?'

'What?! I don't know, my love. There's someone knocking at the door. What time is it?'

'It's still dark. It's four-twenty.' Ângela says this without looking at her watch. Then she glances at her wrist for confirmation – 'Yes, four-twenty. I'm never wrong. Who could it be?'

'I've no idea!'

Ding ding! Ding ding! Knocking. A voice calling. Félix opens the cupboard and takes out a white dressing gown. He puts it on. Ângela gets up.

'Wait.' Her voice is hoarse, a murmur: 'Don't go.'

'I'm going. You wait here.'

I rush across the ceiling. Félix peers out of the living room window. The veranda is in darkness. *Ding ding!!!* He makes his mind up, and opens the door. Edmundo Barata dos Reis hurtles into his arms, pushes him back, closes the door.

'Fucking hell, comrade. They're after me, they're right here. They're going to kill me.'

'Who's going to kill you, damn it?! Explain yourself!'

'Them!'

He's in his underpants. He's barefoot. His U.S.S.R. Communist Party t-shirt seems to have regained some of its original colour – perhaps from the shock. Or maybe it's really blood. Edmundo shakes his grey hair, his eyes bulge from their sockets. He runs from one side of the room to the other. He closes the blinds. Félix watches him, impatient.

'Calm down. Sit down, and calm down. I'll make you some tea.'

He makes for the kitchen. Edmundo follows. He closes the blinds. He closes the window shutters. He sits on a bench, his hands on the table, as Félix puts some water on to boil.

'Soup? Don't you have any soup? I'd rather have some soup…'

Ângela Lúcia appears at the door. She's wearing a man's shirt, blue, very large, which comes down almost to her knees. She must have got it from the cupboard. She has Félix's slippers on her feet, also too big for her. Dressed like that she looks so fragile, almost childlike. Edmundo stumbles:

'I'm sorry, miss – I didn't mean to disturb…'

'What's going on?'

Félix shrugs:

'Edmundo here is going to be killed. Let me introduce you. This is Mr Edmundo Barata dos Reis, ex-agent of the State Security. Or as he'd have it, ex-gent. I've told you about him.'

'Who's going to kill him?!'

'They're going to kill him, and the man wants soup! So… that'll be one soup…'

Ding ding! Ding ding! Ding ding!

Edmundo Barata dos Reis hides his face between his knees. Félix shudders.

'OK, relax. I'll go see who it is. You two just stay here, I'll sort it out. Ângela, don't let him leave.'

He goes back to the living room. He takes a deep breath, and opens the door. In my other life I used to know people like that – they're frightened by the sound of wind through the leaves, they can't bear cockroaches, not to mention policemen, lawyers, even dentists. And yet when the dragon bursts into the clearing, opens its mouth and spits fire, they stand up to them. Calm, cool as an angel.

'What do you want?'

José Buchmann bursts into the room. There's a pistol in his right hand. He's trembling. His voice trembles even more:

'Where is the son of a bitch?'

'First of all, give me that gun. I won't have armed men in my house…'

He says this firmly, without raising his voice, absolutely sure that he will be obeyed. The other man ignores him, though, stepping quickly across the corridor and heading directly for the kitchen. Félix follows him, protesting. I run. I don't want to miss any of the excitement. Ângela Lúcia is standing in the doorway, her arms out, blocking the way:

'You're not coming in!' She explodes: '*Poças!* Where the hell did you come from?'

I can hear the voice of Edmundo Barata dos Reis, shrill, desperate, but only then do I see him. He's standing with his back to the wall, arms hanging down by his sides – his t-shirt glows red on his skinny chest. The blade of the sickle, the gold of the hammer, glimmer for a moment. Then fade.

'Girl, this creature has appeared from hell! From the past! From the place the damned come from…'

José Buchmann is trapped, with Ângela in front of him, and Félix behind him holding his arms. His face is right up against the woman, and he is shouting as though possessed. Suddenly he is like a giant. The veins in his neck fill and pulse, bulge in his forehead:

'Yes, that's right – I've come from the past! And who am I? Well? Tell them who I am!...'

All of a sudden he throws himself forwards, knocking Ângela over while lunging for Edmundo – he grabs his neck with his left hand and forces him to his knees. He pushes the end of the pistol-barrel into his neck:

'Tell them who I am!'

'A ghost. A demon...'

'Who am I!'

'A counter-revolutionary. A spy. An agent of imperialism...'

'What's my name?'

' ... Gouveia. Pedro Gouveia. I should have killed you back in seventy-seven.'

José Buchmann kicks at him. One. Two. Three. Four. Five. He has heavy black boots on, which make a dark sound as they strike the body. Edmundo doesn't cry out. He doesn't even try to avoid the blows. The kicks find his stomach, his chest, his mouth. The boots turn red.

'Shit! Shit!'

José Buchmann – or Pedro Gouveia, as you prefer – puts the pistol down on the table. He takes a cloth and wipes down his boots. He's still shouting – *Shit! Shit!* – as though the other man's blood were burning his feet. Then he sits on a bench, hides his face in his hands, and breaks into a deep, heaving sob, which shakes his whole body. Edmundo Barata dos Reis drags himself to a corner of the kitchen. He sits up, back against the wall, his legs out in front of him. He smiles:

'I never forgot you. I never forgot her either – Marta – young Marta Martinho – passing for some sort of intellectual – poetess, painter and God knows what else. She was pregnant, almost at term, a huge belly. Round. So round. It's as though I can see her now...'

At the door to the corridor, Félix has taken Ângela in his arms, and is watching the scene in silent shock. Pedro Gouveia is crying. I don't know if he's listening to what Edmundo Barata dos Reis is saying. The ex-agent of State Security seems to be enjoying himself. His voice echoes, firm, cold, in the silence of the night:

'It happened a long time ago, didn't it? During the struggles...' He gestures to Ângela – 'The girl hadn't even been born. The Revolution was under threat. There was a band of nobodies, a gang of irresponsible petits-bourgeois who tried to seize power. We had to be tough. *We're not going to waste time on trials*, the Old Man said in his address to the nation, and so we didn't. We did what we had to do. When an orange starts rotting we take it out of the fruit basket and throw it in with the rubbish. If we don't remove it, all the others will rot. One orange is pulled out, or two or three, and the others are saved. That's what we did. Our job was to separate the good oranges from the rotten ones. But this guy – Gouveia – he thought that because he'd been born in Lisbon he'd be able to escape. He phoned the Portuguese consul – *Mr Consul, I'm Portuguese, I'm hiding in such-and-such a place, please come and rescue me, and my wife too, she's a black woman but she's pregnant with my child...* Ha! And do you know what Mr Portuguese Consul did? He went to meet the two of them, then handed them over to me! HA! I thanked him heartily, the consul, I told him he was a true revolutionary – I embraced him – angry though I was, yes, you mustn't think I have no scruples, I'd have preferred to spit in his face, but I embraced him, said goodbye and went off to interrogate the girl. She held out for two days. Then she gave birth – right there – to a little girl, like this, so small; blood, blood – when I think about it all I see is blood... And Mabeco, a mulatto from the South – he died a while ago, a stupid way to go, stabbed twice in cold blood in a bar in Lisbon, they never found out who did it – Mabeco cut the umbilical cord with a penknife, then he lit a cigarette and began to torture the baby, burning it on the back and chest. And the blood! Masses of blood, and the girl, that Marta – her eyes wide like moons – it pains me to dream about it – and the baby screaming, the smell of burning flesh. Even today when I lie down to sleep, the smell is still there, the sound of the child crying...'

'Shut up!'

Félix, a rough shout, a voice I didn't recognise in him. Again:

'Shut up! Shut up!'

From where I'm watching, from here on top of the cupboard, I can see the top of his head lit up in rage – he breaks away from Ângela and advances at Edmundo, fists clenched, shouting:

'Get out of here! Go!'

The ex-agent struggled to his feet, and straightened himself up. He threw a look of disgust at José Buchmann, letting out a harsh laugh:

'Now I'm absolutely certain. It really is you – Gouveia – the factionalist. The other day your laugh almost gave you away. You used to laugh a lot in the faction meetings, before the business with the consul, when your own countryman handed you over to me. Not in prison, though – you just cried in prison. You cried all the time – boohoo, like a girl... I watch you crying now and I see that nobody Gouveia. Revenge – is that what you wanted? No, you need passion for that. You need courage! Killing a man, that's a man's job.'

And then –

     as

          in

              a

                    slow

                          dance...

Ângela crosses the kitchen,
Comes to the table,
her right hand picks up the gun,
her left hand pushes Félix away,
she points at Edmundo's chest –

                  and fires.

The Cry of the Bougainvillea

Out in the yard, where Félix Ventura buried the narrow body of Edmundo Barata dos Reis, now flowers the ruddy glory of a bougainvillea. It grew fast. It's already covering a good part of the wall. It hangs down over the passageway, out there, in a cry of praise – or perhaps of accusation – to which no one pays any heed. A few days ago I summoned up the courage to go out into the yard for the first time. I scaled the wall, my heart pounding. The sun was shining on the shards of glass. I slipped carefully between them, and looked out over the world. I saw a big, wide road, muddy red, with tired old houses cluttering up the other side. People passed by, impervious to the bougainvillea's cries. I was overwhelmed by the vast, cloudless sky, the heavy silence of the light, a flock of birds circling. I hurried back to the safety of the house. Maybe I'll go back out sometime if the weather clouds a bit. The sun dazes me, hurts my skin, but I would like to take a more leisurely look at those people passing…

Félix has been sad. He's hardly been talking to me. But today he broke his silence. He came into the house, took off his dark glasses, put them away in the inside pocket of his jacket, then took the jacket off and hung it on the back of a chair. Then he opened a folder and took out a small square yellow envelope.

'Another photo has arrived – you see, my friend? She still hasn't forgotten us.'

He opened the envelope with great care, trying not to tear it. A Polaroid. A river lit up by a rainbow. In the top right-hand corner, you could make out the silhouette of a naked youth diving into the water. In the margin, Ângela Lúcia had written in blue ink: *Plácidas Águs, Pará*, and the date. Félix went to get a little box of pins, those little ones with coloured round heads. He chose one, a bright, ludicrous green, and fixed the photograph to the wall. Then he took three steps back to consider the effect. The living room wall facing the window is now almost completely covered in photographs. All together they make up a kind of stained-glass window; it reminds me of David Hockney's experiments with Polaroids. Shades of blue predominate.

Félix Ventura turned the big wicker chair towards the wall and sat down. He spent some time there, motionless, silent, watching the fine evening light dying as it met the immortal light of the Polaroids. His eyes filled with tears. With a handkerchief he wiped them away. Then he said:

'I know. You want me to forgive her. I'm so sorry my friend, but I can't. I don't think I can do it.'

The Man in the Mask

The man who has just walked in reminds me of someone. But I still haven't been able to work out who. Tall, elegant, well dressed. His grey hair, cropped short, gives him an air of nobility, an air which his broad, rather coarse face quickly dispels. I watch him make his way across the sleeping evening light, as a tiger. He ignores the hand Félix proffers him, and then – apparently a little bored – sits down with legs crossed on the leather sofa. He sighs deeply. His fingers drum on the sofa's arm.

'I'm going to tell you an improbable story. I'm going to tell you because I know you won't believe me. I'd like to trade this improbable story, the story of my life, for another story – one that's simple, and solid. The story of an ordinary man. I'll give you an impossible truth, and you give me a vulgar and believable lie – OK?'

He'd started well. Interested, Félix sat down.

'You see this face?' The man pointed to his face with both hands. 'Well, it's not mine.'

A long pause. He hesitated. Then at last he began:

'They stole my face. Oh... how can I explain this to you? They stole me from myself. I woke up one day to discover that they'd done plastic surgery on me, and left me in a clinic with an envelope full of dollars and a postcard: *We thank you for the services rendered – consider your job done.* That's what it said on the postcard. They could have killed me. I don't know why they didn't kill me. Maybe they thought that this way I'm even deader... Or rather, that's what I thought at first, that they wanted me to suffer. And I did, those first days I really did suffer. I considered reporting what had

167

happened. I sought out my friends. Some of them didn't believe me. Others did believe me, in spite of the mask I now wear, because after all I know certain things – but they pretended not to believe me. I thought it would be dangerous to insist. And then one evening, an evening like this one, sitting alone at a table outside a bar at the end of the Island, I began to enjoy an amazing sensation – I wasn't sure what to call it; but I do know now, it was Freedom! I'd been transformed into a free man. I had funds, I had access to accounts abroad that would see me out for the rest of my life. And I had the weight of no responsibilities – no critics, no remorse, no envy, no hatred, no rancour, no court intrigue, still less any fear that one day someone would betray me...'

Félix Ventura shakes his head, troubled:

'I used to know someone – he was crazy, one of those unfortunates you find wandering around the city, getting in the way of the traffic, and he had a very strange theory. He believed that the President had been replaced by a double. Your story reminds me of that...'

The man looked at him, curious. His voice became more gentle, almost dream-like:

'All stories are connected. In the end everything is connected.' A sigh. 'But only a few lunatics – very few of them, and they do have to be very crazy indeed – are able to understand this. Anyway. What I'm after is for you to arrange for me exactly the opposite of what you usually do for people – I want you to give me a modest past. A name with no lustre to it whatsoever. A genealogy that is obscure, and irrefutable. There must be men who are rich but who have no family and no glory, surely? I want to be like that...'

Dream No. 6

A very tall cage rose up in front of us, broad and deep, out of which from time to time, in faint gusts, burst the happy chirping of birds. Parakeets, waxbills, Long-tailed Tyrants, *peitos-celestes*, touracos, turtledoves, bee-eaters. We were sitting on well-worn plastic chairs, in the fragrant shade of a leafy mango tree. To our left ran a low brick wall, painted white. Hugely tall papaya trees laden with fruit swayed beside the wall, languid as a mulatto woman. Looking over to the right, towards the house, were ranks of orange trees, lime trees, guava trees. Further still was a massive baobab which dominated the orchard. It looked as though it had been put there just to remind me that this was no more than a dream. Pure fiction. Chickens pecked away at the red earth, and in the very green grass, dragging their broods of chicks behind them. José Buchmann gave me a clear smile of victory.

'Welcome to my humble domain.'

He clapped his hands and a slender, shy girl in a short little dress and plastic sandals appeared from the gloom. Buchmann asked her to bring a cold beer for him, a *pitanga* juice for me. Without a word the girl lowered her head, and vanished. Not long afterwards she returned balancing a bottle of beer, two glasses and a jug with the juice, on a tray. Mistrustfully I tasted the juice. It was good, bitter and sweet all at once, very fresh, with a fragrance that could light up even the gloomiest soul.

'We're in Chibia — but you know that already, don't you? However much I thank our dear common friend Félix for having invented this land for me, I can never thank him enough.'

'Excuse my curiosity. Is there really a plot, in a cemetery near here somewhere, with the name Mateus Buchmann on it?'

'There is. A lot of the plots had been destroyed, among them – and why not? – my father's. I had the stone made myself. You saw it. You did see the photograph, didn't you?'

'I understand. And Eva Miller's watercolours?'

'I really did find those at an antique-dealer's, in Cape Town – a fabulous shop that sold a bit of everything, jewels and photo albums, right through to old cameras. Eva Miller is a common enough name. There must be several dozen watercolourists in the world with that name. The brief notice of her death that appeared in the Johannesburg *Século*, yes, I did make that one up – with the help of an old Portuguese typesetter friend of mine. I needed Félix himself to believe in my life story. If he believed it, who wouldn't? And today, I honestly believe it myself. I look back now, back into my past, and I see two lives. In one, I was Pedro Gouveia, in another José Buchmann. Pedro Gouveia died. José Buchmann returned to Chibia.'

'And did you know that Ângela was your daughter?'

'Yes, I knew. I left prison in nineteen-eighty. I was destroyed, totally destroyed – physically, morally, psychologically. Edmundo took me to the airport, put me on a plane and sent me to Portugal. There was no one waiting for me there. I didn't have family there any more, or at least none that I knew of, I had nothing left, no connection at all. My mother – poor woman – had died in Luanda while I was in prison. My father had been living in Rio de Janeiro for years with another woman. I'd never had much contact with him. Yes, I had been born in Lisbon, but I'd gone to Luanda when I was tiny, even before I'd learned to talk. Portugal was my country, they told me, they told me so in prison – the other prisoners, the informers – but I never felt Portuguese. I stayed in Lisbon for two or three years, working as a copy-editor on a weekly paper. It was then, through my contact with the photographers working on the paper, that I began to get interested in photography. I did a quick course, and set off for Paris. From there, I went to Berlin. I began working as a photo-journalist, and spent years – decades – crossing the world from war to war, trying to forget myself. I earned a lot of money – a lot, really – but didn't know what to do with it all. Nothing appealed to me. My whole life was an attempt to escape. Then one evening I found myself in Lisbon – one of those in-between places on the map. In a restaurant in Restauradores, where I'd gone in attracted by the smell of chicken giblets like my mother used to make, I came across an old comrade of mine. He was the first person to tell me about Ângela. That son of a bitch – Edmundo – had derived great pleasure telling me every time he interrogated me of how he'd killed my wife. He told me they'd murdered the baby too. But it turned out they hadn't killed her. They'd handed her over to Marina, Marta's sister, and she had brought her up. She'd brought her up as though she were her own daughter. I was disturbed when I heard this. Years had passed, and I'd grown old. I wanted to know my daughter, to spend time with her, but I didn't have the courage to tell her the truth. I became obsessed. I was overcome by hatred, by a savage bitterness towards those people, towards Edmundo. I wanted to kill him. I thought that if I killed him I'd be able to look my daughter in the eye. Perhaps if I killed him, I would be reborn. I returned to Luanda, with no clear idea of what I was going to do. I was afraid of being recognised. On a table in the bar of my hotel I found a business card for our friend Félix Ventura. *Give your children a better past.* Excellent paper. Very well printed. That was when I had the idea of contracting his services – with another identity it would be easier for me to move around the city without arousing suspicion. I could kill Edmundo, and disappear. But I wanted him to know why he was going to die, I wanted to confront him with his crimes – deep down, yes, I know that I wanted revenge. It was hard to find him, and when I did track him down I discovered that he'd gone mad. Or at least, he seemed that way. I went with him to Félix's house because I wanted to hear someone else's opinion of the matter – and Félix thought that – yes – Edmundo was mad. At that point I almost gave up. I couldn't kill a madman. Then one evening I waited for him to leave the sewer where he used to hide out, and I slipped down into it. And there, in that filthy hole, I found a mattress, dirty clothes, magazines, Marxist literature and – would you believe it? – a set of archives containing the State Security reports for dozens of people. My case was one of the first. And that's where I was, with a torch in one hand and the file in the other – thrilled, confused – when all of a sudden Edmundo appeared, like a soul condemned. He jumped in from the gutter, landing two paces from me. He had a knife in his hand. He was laughing. My God, that laugh! He said: *The two of us, face to face again, comrade Pedro*

Gouveia – but this time I'm going to finish you off… – and he lunged at me. I kicked him away, drew a gun from my belt – I'd bought the gun just days earlier at Roque Santeiro, believe it or not – and fired. The bullet hit his chest, just grazed it; I dropped the torch, dropped everything, in a panic, and he scrabbled up the hole. I grabbed his legs, held fast, but he shook, wriggled, freed himself, leaving me holding his trousers. I chased after him. The rest you know. You were there. You witnessed everything that happened after that.'

'And what about Ângela – did she know you were her father?'

'Yes, she swears she did. She told me that Marina had kept our tragedy hidden from her for years. Until one day – it was bound to happen – someone or other – a classmate, I think, someone from her university – dropped a hint. Ângela reacted very badly. She was furious with Marina and her husband – her parents, her real parents, after all – both wonderful people. She was furious with them, and left Angola. She went to London. She went to New York. She'd learned that I was a photographer, and this led to her becoming interested in photography. She became a photographer, like me; and, like me, she became a nomad. And a few months ago you noticed the coincidence that we were both photographers and both returned to the country at about the same time – and you didn't believe it was a coincidence. Well, as you see it wasn't entirely coincidence. Ângela swears that the moment she saw me, that night – you remember, that night in your house? – the moment she saw me, the moment she set eyes on me, she guessed who I was. I don't know. When I think about that moment, all I remember is the shock of it. It was such a strange meeting for me. I did know who she was. Neither of us said a word. We just sat in silence. Months went by, until that evening when I shot at Edmundo, and he ran for refuge with the only person who could take him in – Félix Ventura, former student of Professor Gaspar, one of his tribe…'

José Buchmann was quiet. He drank down what was left of his beer in a long draught, and then sat, absorbed, his eyes lost in the dense foliage of the mango tree. The big orchard suited him. The shade fell across us like a burst of fresh water. For a moment the rough passion of cicadas added to the singing of the birds. A drowsiness came over me, I wanted to shut my eyes and sleep, but I resisted it, sure that if I fell asleep moments later I would awake transformed into a gecko.

'Have you had news from Ângela?'

'Yes, I hear from her. At this moment she should be going down the Amazon on a big, lazy, slow-boat, one of those boats that at night-time they cover with hammocks. There's a lot of sky there. A lot of light in the water. I hope she's happy.'

'And what about you – are you happy?'

'I'm at peace, at last. I fear nothing, I yearn for nothing. I suppose you could call that happiness. Do you know what Aldous Huxley used to say? *Happiness is never grand.*'

'And what will become of you now?'

'Oh, I've no idea. I'll probably be a grandfather.'

Félix Ventura Begins to Keep a Diary

This morning I found Eulálio dead. Poor Eulálio. He'd fallen at the foot of my bed, with an enormous scorpion, a horrible creature, also dead, clamped between his teeth. He died in combat, like a hero – Eulálio, who'd never thought of himself as courageous. I buried him in the yard, shrouded in a silk handkerchief, one of my best handkerchiefs, beside the trunk of the avocado tree. I chose the side of the tree facing the setting sun, damp and covered in moss, because it's always shady there. Like me, Eulálio never liked the sun. I'll miss him. I decided to start keeping this diary today, to maintain the illusion that there's someone listening to me. I'll never have another listener like him, though. He was my best friend, I think. I suppose I'll stop meeting him in my dreams now. And indeed with every passing day, every passing hour, my memory of him becomes more and more like a figure made of sand. The memory of a dream. Maybe I dreamed it all: him, José Buchmann, Edmundo Barata dos Reis. I dare not dig up the yard, there beside the bougainvillea, in case I find nothing there – the possibility terrifies me. As for Ângela Lúcia, if I did dream her, I dreamed her very well. The postcards she still sends me, one every three or four days, are almost real. I bought an immense map of the world, bought it online from Altair. Altair in Barcelona is my favourite bookshop. Whenever I go to Barcelona I set aside two or three days to lose myself in Altair, consulting books and maps and photo albums and planning journeys I will take one day; and above all planning all those journeys I never will take. I've hung the map on the living room wall, fixed to a corkboard, next to Ângela Lúcia's Polaroids. Each of her postcards bears a note mentioning where the picture was taken, so it's easy for me to track her progress (I've pierced each place with a green-headed pin). I can see that Ângela went down the Amazon as far as Belém do Pará. By my reckoning she then rented a car – or took a bus, more likely – heading southward. From São Luís do Maranhão she sent me the flaming silhouette of a little square-sailed boat: *Anil River, February 9th*. Four days later I received the image of a child's hand throwing a paper aeroplane. There's a river slipping past in the background, fat and grey under the slow sun: *Ilhas Canárias, Parnaíba Delta, February 13th*. It's not hard for me to imagine where she'll go in the coming days. Yesterday I bought a ticket for Rio de Janeiro. The day after tomorrow I fly from Santos Dumont airport to Fortaleza. I don't think it will be hard for me to find her. If José Buchmann was able to find a fellow countryman, an *accorentado*, inside a phone box in Berlin, with no point of reference but a traffic light, it'll be even quicker for me to find a woman who loves to photograph clouds. I don't know what I'll do when I find her. I hope that you, my good Eulálio, will help me to make the right decision. I'm an animist. I've always been an animist, though I've only lately realised it. The same thing happens to the soul as happens to water – it flows. Today it's a river. Tomorrow, it will be the sea. Water takes the shape of whatever receives it. Inside a bottle it's like a bottle. But it isn't a bottle. Eulálio will always be Eulálio, whether flesh (incarnate) or fish. I'm reminded of that black and white picture of Martin Luther King speaking to the crowd: *I have a dream...* He really should have said 'I *made* a dream'. If you think about it there's a difference between having a dream and *making* a dream.

Yes, I've made a dream.

Lisbon, February 13th, 2004.